Seducing the Duchess

Disgraceful Duchesses, Book 1

Sara Bennett

ARE YOU SIGNED UP FOR DRAGONBLADE'S BLOG?

You'll get the latest news and information on exclusive giveaways, exclusive excerpts, coming releases, sales, free books, cover reveals and more.

Check out our complete list of authors, too!

No spam, no junk. That's a promise!

Sign Up Here

www.dragonbladepublishing.com

Dearest Reader;

Thank you for your support of a small press. At Dragonblade Publishing, we strive to bring you the highest quality Historical Romance from some of the best authors in the business. Without your support, there is no 'us', so we sincerely hope you adore these stories and find some new favorite authors along the way.

Happy Reading!

CEO, Dragonblade Publishing

Prologue

London, 1808

THE BALLROOM WAS full of chattering, important people. Nineteen-year-old Catherine Mallory felt rather over-whelmed, but she was doing her best to enjoy herself. She had lately become engaged to the Duke of Winstanton, who planned for them to make their home at his castle in the north. Catherine knew—he told her at least once a day—that he was not fond of London.

She had only been part of the social scene for three months, barely any time at all, and now she was to be married. Her sister Sophia, at seventeen, was longing to join in the balls and parties, while fifteen-year-old Ellis preferred to curl up in bed with her book. It was Catherine who led the way, as her mother liked to remind them. She blazed a trail for her sisters to follow, one of grand marriages and more money than they knew what to do with, as that was Mrs. Mallory's vision of success. They had been as poor as church mice when they left their village in Hampshire, after accepting the kind offer of Mrs. Mallory's cousin to introduce them into society. Despite Catherine's beautiful face and serene nature, no one had quite expected her to unleash such a storm among the *ton*. There had been several flattering proposals, but the duke's was the pick of them.

If only he weren't so *old*. Catherine tried not to sigh, because Winstanton was very old indeed, and she found the thought of him touching her, kissing her, repugnant. Most of the time she tried not to think about it at all.

"He'll probably die in a year or two," Sophia had said with a callous shrug. "You'll just have to put up with it. Unless you find yourself a handsome lover."

Sometimes her sister seemed far less innocent than Catherine knew her to be.

A deep chuckle caught her attention, and she looked about for its owner. A tall, fair-haired gentleman stood with a group of ladies, his smile both charming and mischievous. He chuckled again, and several of the ladies giggled. *This* was the sort of man she had naively believed she would marry. Young and handsome, like the hero in one of Ellis' books. But then life wasn't like a story in a book.

"That's Albury," the duke hissed in her ear.

Catherine started and turned to look at him. "Albury?"

"Viscount Sebastian Albury. His father is the Earl of Eltham, and his mother . . ." Winstanton's already thin mouth tightened until it was almost lipless. "She was killed in an accident in a gig. Albury was driving."

"How dreadful," Catherine whispered. Although, watching Albury now, he didn't appear to have suffered from the experience. She hadn't meant to speak the words aloud, but she must have, because the duke took her arm and turned her away from the handsome viscount. He shot her a reproving look.

"Albury might be young, but he is already bidding to be a rake. A heartless lecher." He pronounced the word with relish, and added a nod when Catherine gasped. "Since the earl banished him, Albury spends his days drinking and carousing."

The words were shocking, but when she turned her head again she was even more shocked to see that Albury was now standing right behind them. He had no doubt heard his personal business being discussed so freely, as anger made his pale blue eyes blaze before they cooled and he settled his features into a bland smile. Catherine supposed he'd had lots of practice shrugging off gossip, and even if he was as guilty as the duke said, she still felt sorry for him. Catherine, too, had been the subject of gossip and knew how painful it could be.

Albury met her gaze, and she could see the spark of interest in their pale depths. She was used to being ogled and called "exquisite," and in the beginning it had turned her head a little. Not anymore. She had soon discovered that these people weren't interested in what she thought or how she felt, only in how she looked. After her amazing rise from poor country girl to a duke's intended, they seemed to think that by being in her company some of her good fortune would rub off on them.

"Winstanton," the viscount said loudly, with the slightest of bows.

Catherine was amused to see the duke jump in surprise before he spun about. She held a gloved hand up to her mouth to muffle a nervous giggle. Albury's gaze was on her again, and the mischief she had noticed earlier returned to his handsome face.

"Who is this gorgeous creature?" he asked. "Do introduce us."

Catherine felt her cheeks heat. It was the way he was looking at her. She had been looked at a great deal over the past three months, but no one had done so with such a warm, teasing smile.

The duke's face pinched as if he'd sucked on a lemon. "This is my future wife, Miss Catherine Mallory. And I will thank you to keep a civil tongue in your head, Albury."

Catherine noticed he didn't introduce the viscount to her, a slight that couldn't have gone unnoticed. Albury took it in his stride, bowing in her direction now, while those icy blue eyes swept over her in a manner that was anything but icy.

"But of course! The beautiful Miss Mallory. I had heard there were a great many gentlemen vying for her hand. And you are the lucky fellow who won her, Winstanton? I presume it was your wit and charm that did the trick."

Despite his words verging on insult, the droll note in his voice took away the sting. Besides, there was that teasing sparkle in his eyes that seemed to invite her to join with him in laughing at the ridiculousness of it all. Catherine suspected Viscount Albury did not take life very seriously.

Winstanton wasn't listening. "As soon as I saw her, I had to have her. She has the sort of beauty one rarely sees." He had spoken like this before, as though she weren't even present, and Catherine found it embarrassing.

"Ah yes, I recall you are a great collector of beautiful things." Now Albury was looking at him cooly. The next moment he turned that charming smile again on Catherine. "The duke and my father are neighbors, if one can call a journey of a full day a neighborly distance."

Hope lit inside her. "Oh. Then perhaps we will see you at the castle?"

Albury laughed but there was no humor in it. "I rarely visit, I'm afraid. London has so much more to offer."

Winstanton was staring at Catherine, and she wondered if he had heard a word of the conversation. He nodded, as if in reply to some thought of his own. "She will be the prize of my collection."

The viscount and Catherine exchanged glances.

"Your collection?" Albury repeated. "I thought your obsession was pottery, Winstanton. Miss Mallory does not look like a vase to me."

Catherine almost giggled again but swallowed it down when the duke shot her a warning look. "My collection comprises many beautiful pieces."

Albury frowned, as if the duke's words troubled him. "It sounds like you plan to put Miss Mallory upon a shelf and leave her there." He gave a slight shake of his head and leaned toward her, his voice no more than a whisper in her ear.

"You could always run away with me."

Her eyes widened. Albury wanted to run away with her? He

was joking, surely? Yes, now he winked at her, so he was not being serious. Her heart did a little dive of disappointment, but even as she reminded herself how much was riding on her triumphant marriage, running away had seemed—just for a moment—like the perfect plan.

"Damned cheek," the duke muttered. "What did he say, Catherine? Tell me at once."

She didn't answer, watching Albury walk away, his broad shoulders swaying and his long legs eating up the floor.

"I'm glad we will be leaving immediately after the wedding," Winstanton went on, his vicelike clutch on her arm making her wince. "You will have plenty to occupy you once we get to Winstanton."

And Viscount Albury is our neighbor.

Perhaps he read the words in her head because her future husband gave a grimly satisfied smile. "And don't worry about Albury. He never leaves London. You will not see him again."

Chapter One

1818: Ten years later

CATHERINE TURNED OVER in bed and stared at the window. The snow was still coming down, just as it had been yesterday, when they had found shelter at the White Rose Inn. She had been returning from a visit to London to see her mother and sisters and should be home by now at Winstanton Castle. Instead, she was a prisoner of the weather, and her feelings about that were ambivalent.

On the one hand, she was longing to see her son, Jack, who was five years old. He was waiting for her at the castle and there was no one in the world she loved more than Jack. On the other hand, the weather had given her a brief reprieve from a life she had grown to hate. Winstanton had been her home for the past ten years, but it had never really felt like *her* home, and being away for even a brief time had reminded her just how true that was.

The Winstanton Estate was mostly moor and crags, the castle a grim piece of architecture from the 1600s. Built to keep the Scots out and the family in, as her late husband, the Duke of Winstanton, used to say. She had hated it from the moment she'd set eyes on it. And even now that she was the Dowager Duchess of Winstanton she could never leave that depressing place, because her late husband had written a specific clause into his will stating that if she did leave to make a happier life elsewhere, then she could not take Jack, his only heir, with her.

My estate and monies go to my son, Alfred Algernon Jonathon, in the guardianship of my sister Ellinor. He will live at Winstanton until he turns twenty-one, when he will assume control of said estate and monies. My wife, Catherine, may remain at Winstanton with my son, but only if she continues in a single state. If she remarries, then she must leave. Furthermore, if she makes her home away from Winstanton, she can neither take my son with her nor can he visit her. In short, Catherine cannot remove my son from Winstanton. If she ignores my wishes, then my son will no longer inherit my estate and monies, which will be given over to the British Museum.

It had been a terrible shock when Catherine was informed of the late duke's stipulations regarding her future. The marriage had not been a happy one, but she had tried to be a good wife to him. She'd helped Ellinor run his household and had seen to his care as he'd grown more feeble. Had that counted for nothing? He still could not let go of her, keeping her his prisoner even after death.

Ellinor had not been surprised. The duke's sister had lived her whole life at Winstanton, so she expected the same of Jack and Catherine. She was some twenty years younger than her brother, and a quiet mouse of a woman, intent upon obeying her dead brother's wishes to the letter. Catherine would get no support from her if she tried to rebel against the will.

Tired of her depressing thoughts, Catherine pushed aside the covers and sat up. The floor beside the bed was cold and her toes felt like ice. She shivered as she slipped her feet into her slippers. Where was Maggie, her maid? Probably chatting with the inn's groom—the two of them seemed to hit it off when they arrived last night, and Maggie was an unrepentant flirt. Catherine didn't mind. Maggie might have her faults, but she was full of the joy of life and lifted Catherine's spirits whenever she was down in the dumps.

And Catherine could forgive her anything when she remembered first arriving at the castle, feeling frightened and alone, only to be greeted by Maggie's warm, compassionate smile. It had been like a balm to her aching heart.

"Never you mind," Maggie had crooned as Catherine lay sobbing after the duke had paid another visit to her bedchamber. "It won't always be like this. One day you'll find a man to make your heart sing."

Catherine had yet to find that man. Her ten years of marriage had definitely not been the stuff of romance novels. And now she was a widow at nine and twenty years, alone with her young son in their icy fortress, and uncertain how she was ever going to escape. During her visit to London, her mother had talked of Catherine making another marriage. Adding another glittering coronet to the one she already had.

"Pooh! What matters it if you lose Winstanton?" she had said. "There are plenty of other prospects, and you are still beautiful. And Jack will thank you for helping him to escape that awful place."

But would he? As Ellinor had pointed out to her when the will was read and Catherine had protested, Jack would still be a duke, but the title would be an empty one. And what would he think as he grew older and understood what his mother's selfish actions had stolen from him? His birthright, a fortune, and a castle. Catherine doubted he would thank her, and how could she be happy if Jack hated her?

But it was pointless trying to explain that to Ellen Mallory. She only believed what she wanted to and thought that Catherine's happiness had been a fair trade for a coronet. But the truth was that one miserable marriage was enough. As bleak as Winstanton was, Catherine would prefer to live in that castle in the north rather than alienate her son for the sake of some man who may be no better than her late husband.

With a huff of impatience—why was she wallowing in yet more dismaying thoughts?—she reached for her fur-lined cloak and wrapped it over her nightgown. She needed to find flirtatious Maggie, and then partake of breakfast. Perhaps if the road wasn't as bad as it had been yesterday—*impassable* the innkeeper had called it last night—Catherine might still be able to complete her journey. It was only another two days to Winstanton, or probably three when one considered their antiquated coach.

The stairs creaked as she descended. She could smell wood fires and food cooking, both adding to the stuffy, smoky atmosphere. There was a murmur of voices toward the back of the inn, and she hesitated in the passage at the bottom of the staircase, wondering if she should just go back to her room and wait. The duke had often accused her of behaving thoughtlessly. But why, a year after he had died, was she still listening to his reproving voice in her head?

Her gaze went to the front door. It was closed, though she could see the bolt had been drawn back. What she needed was a lungful of crisp, cold air. Catherine hurried to the door.

It was solid and heavy-looking, and she had expected to have difficulty in opening it, but instead it swung open so easily on its oiled hinges that she was forced to step back.

Just as someone pushed through from the outside in a flurry of snow-dusted clothing and collided with her.

Strong arms wrapped around her to save her from falling, and she had the impression of a tall, muscular body. Her cloak slipped from her shoulders and puddled onto the floor. He must have taken off his gloves, because his hands felt warm on her skin through her thin nightgown. One of them was pressed into her upper back, and the other closed on her bottom, curving about one soft, rounded cheek.

Catherine gave a squeak of surprise. Briefly her face was squished against the rough wool of his coat, and her senses reeled from the scents of warm male and citrus pomade. Her hands flew to his chest, as she tried to push herself away, but lingered instead on a body comprised of flesh and hard muscle.

They were only in the doorway together for a moment,

though it felt much longer. When she finally wrestled herself free of his supporting hands, her hair had come loose from its braid, and the straps on her nightgown had slipped, so that the tip of one breast was peeking over the neckline. She quickly righted herself, but he must have seen as he stooped to collect her cloak.

"There," he said in a deep voice, unexpectedly warm with humor, as he wrapped it securely about her shoulders. "Now you are respectable again."

Breathlessly, she looked up at the assailant.

Before her stood a tall gentleman in a many-caped coat, shoulders dusted with snow and hair so fair it was almost white. Appreciative pale blue eyes stared down upon her, fire from their encounter lingering in their depths. His face was strong and handsome, with a chiselled jaw and a bold, straight nose, while amusement twitched at the corners of a generous mouth.

And she knew him!

Shockingly, it was a face she recognized despite the years. He was older, and there were lines at the corners of his eyes, but he was in essence the same man. As if to put the matter beyond doubt, those long-ago words echoed in her head.

You could always run away with me.

The man in front of her smiled, and she wagered his lips would be as soft as they looked if she pressed her own to them. Before he devoured her. And he looked like he wanted to devour her right now.

"Apologies for manhandling you, madam. Are you harmed?"

He did not recognize her. Why was that so painful? Catherine managed a shake of her head, as with trembling hands she pulled her cloak even closer. His blue eyes slid over her in that same brash way she remembered, and her skin prickled. She was very aware of her nakedness beneath the nightdress. His hands on her body had left an imprint—the squeeze of her buttock, the press of her face to his chest.

"Is the road clear yet?" she asked, her voice oddly breathless.

He was watching her as he brushed snow from his shoulders

and stamped it from his boots. "Unfortunately not. I was hoping for a room to wait out the worst of the weather."

No, he didn't recognize her. Why should he? Just because Viscount Albury inhabited her dreams, that did not mean he ever thought of her. As her husband had pointed out to her all those years ago, Albury was a rake, a gentleman with many conquests to his name. Why should he remember their brief conversation just because she did?

She looked up again to find that now he was frowning at her in a puzzled way. He opened his mouth but before he could say whatever he meant to say, heavy footsteps approached from the passage behind her, and the innkeeper's hearty voice boomed out. "Welcome, welcome, good sir! Welcome to The White Rose."

Albury caught Catherine's eye with a lift of his eyebrows and an amused quirk to his lips, before stepping past her.

It was a relief to have his attention turned elsewhere, but Catherine's head was a jumble of thoughts and emotions, and she needed to be alone to sort through them. As the two men spoke, she slipped through the front door, closing it behind her. There was a smart equipage sitting in the yard, a far more modern coach than her own, and one of the stable boys was holding the heads of the steaming horses.

Her body still tingled from contact with his. She had always known Viscount Albury was the sort of man who made sensible women behave in ways that were anything but sensible. Why else, after one meeting, had Catherine never forgotten him? She shivered, and it wasn't from the cold. Catherine had long dreamed of a man like him, one who knew how to give a woman pleasure. An expert in quenching a thirst for passion.

Ten years of longing welled up inside her and she stumbled to a halt, her hand clenched in her cloak, the cold air stinging her throat as she tried to breathe. She felt overwhelmed. The stables were to her left, the doors were open, and she could hear Maggie's laughter, but she stayed put.

Meeting Albury here, again, after all this time, seemed . . . miraculous. Like a wish come true. She knew the road to the north would eventually open and she would go on her way, and so would he. They may be neighbors, but they would never meet again. She would stay in her castle, and he would return to London. But right now, right this moment, they were here. Together.

She had yearned for someone with whom to share her bed. A man who could show her all that she had been missing. And her dream man had always worn Albury's face from that long ago evening in London. She hadn't expected him to look the same, and he didn't. He was older with a certain world-weary air about him. But instead of that dissuading her, it only increased her desire for him.

Catherine made a sound between a laugh and a sob and covered her mouth with her hands. For ten years she had been waiting for a moment like this, and now it was here.

Chapter Two

THE INNKEEPER HAD recognized Sebastian as one of the Quality and was effusive in his desire to help in any way he could. "Arnold Rose at your service, sir. I see you are surprised by my name. There have been Roses at The White Rose for centuries." Seb listened to his assurances that yes, of course there was a room, and it was cleaned and ready. By the time Seb thought to glance behind him, the front door was closed and the woman was gone.

That moment in the doorway didn't seem quite real. Her face. He knew it, he knew *her*, but the memory eluded him. Her dark hair had been tumbling about her after their scuffle, and the way she had gazed up at him with her large dark eyes . . . she seemed to know him, too. When was the last time a face had captivated him so immediately and so completely? The feel of her body against his, brief as it had been, had brought his flagging amorousness back to vivid life.

Good God, he could still feel the soft flesh of her bottom in the curve of his hand and see the taut bud of her nipple where her breast had escaped its confinement. His body had roared into life in a way it hadn't for a long time now. He was cock struck— aching within the confines of his breeches—and all because of a stranger's pretty face.

"Sir? I hope there is a room." Dodds had arrived at his side. His manservant's hazel eyes flicked between Seb and the innkeeper. "A night out in this weather would freeze my balls off." Dodds usually said what he thought, and that appealed to Seb—there were too many toadeaters in his world.

"There is a room for me. You have a cupboard," Seb responded dryly.

"Wonderful," Dodds muttered.

They followed the innkeeper up the creaky staircase, Dodds carrying Seb's case. "There's a very attractive maid by the name of Maggie staying here," he said at Seb's shoulder. "I met her just now. I don't think she'd say no to wiling away some time together."

Dodds had a way with women. They found his ex-boxer's face alluring rather than ugly, and his strong, compact body desirable. Had the woman at the door been Maggie? The idea of his manservant trying his luck with her did not sit well with Seb, and he knew why. He wanted her for himself.

The innkeeper spoke up, having overheard the conversation. "That'll be the duchess' maid."

"Duchess?" Seb asked, as the man opened the door to their room with a flourish. It was basic but clean, and he had been promised hot water to wash in before breakfast was served.

Dodds looked about with a frown, as if the place was not up to his standards. "Is there a private parlor?"

"Indeed there is! But only the one, I'm afraid. You'll have to share with the other guests." Rose made a moue which belied the sparkle in his eyes. The snow might be bad luck for the travelers, but it was obviously a windfall for the inn.

Dodds wasn't appeased. "Viscount Albury is not used to eating with any old Tom, Dick, and Harry."

"We will manage," Seb said quickly, before Dodds could create a fuss and lose them the room altogether. For some reason his servant considered it his job to draw attention to his master's consequence.

Dodds grunted and found a coin from the purse he kept about him for just such occasions as this. He handed it to the smiling innkeeper and closed the door.

"How much did you give him?" Seb asked, going to stand at the window. It overlooked the back of the inn, where there was an expanse of forest with bare trees, their branches laden with snow.

"A shilling," Dodds said, with disdain. "I'm sure the duchess has the best room, so he doesn't deserve more."

The forest reminded Seb of the wood at Albury House. His home. He remembered playing there as a boy and planting new trees with his father with their own hands when a storm had uprooted several old ones. "You'll be able to sit in their shade when *your* son is grown," he had said. His father was normally busy managing the estate, and those times with just the two of them had been precious. Then his mother died, tragically, and Seb and his father had had that terrible argument. Despite the time that had passed, the memory was perfectly clear, and perfectly painful. Afterward, Seb had marched out of the house and ridden away to London, where he had made his life. Money left to him by his grandfather had ensured he was comfortable, and Seb was not one to throw away his pennies at the gambling clubs. He and his father had not exchanged a word or a letter since that day.

Until a week ago when he received an urgent message from old Grimsley, the butler at Albury.

Come home. Your father is ill. He needs you.

Seb had read that short missive many times since. It sounded like his father was dying. Did he want to see him again before the end? Was there any point in trying to repair the fracture in their relationship after what had been said? Probably not, and yet he had set off anyway.

London-born Dodds had complained during their journey north—or to the "godless north" as he was apt to say. True, it wasn't the best time of year to be traveling, but the winter was meant to be over. Although the spring was always slower to arrive up here, the heavy snowfall and the storm that brought it had still been unexpected. Thinking he had no time to waste, Albury had journeyed through the night, but they had made slow progress, and by dawn it was obvious it would be too perilous to go on. The White Rose made the perfect stopping place until the weather improved.

The sight of the bare trees beyond his window had brought back memories, good memories, and despite Seb's confused emotions when it came to his father, he was glad he was here. Another day or two and the road would be passable again, and he could go home.

"Who is this duchess?" he asked Dodds belatedly.

"Dowager Duchess," his manservant corrected him, as he began to set out fresh clothing for Seb to change into after he had washed. "Her husband died a year ago, and she is just out of mourning. Not that he was worth the effort, according to Maggie. Nasty piece of work. He forced her to live in a drafty old castle and even though he's dead she still can't leave if she wants to hang on to the money."

Seb turned to stare at him. It couldn't be! Could it . . .? "Was the name 'Winstanton' by any chance?"

Dodds eyed him cautiously. "Sounded like it. Do you know her? One of your conquests, is she?"

Catherine Mallory—the name came to him at last, and with it their meeting in London. There had been a connection between them, a sparkle in her eyes when they caught his, as if she perfectly understood and enjoyed his dry wit. All the same, she had been seriously out of her depth, and he'd had the foolish and uncharacteristic urge to rescue her. Though of course he hadn't. He had never been a hero, and he doubted she had wanted to be rescued when she was on the verge of becoming a wealthy duchess. But for whatever reason her beautiful face had stayed with him for a long time after, and even now when he had thought her forgotten, he remembered her.

"No," he said in answer to Dodds' question. "Quite the opposite, actually."

She had not been a conquest then, but what about now? Would she be open to the suggestion? He thought himself a little mad to consider it, but that moment with her in his arms had turned him reckless. And it had been a very long time since Seb had desired a woman like this.

Dodds waited a moment but when Seb said no more, he announced he was going to see about the hot water.

With the room to himself, Seb turned again to the window. It was odd enough that he remembered those brief moments with Catherine Mallory, but he hadn't been mistaken—she had remembered him, too. And now they were together in this inn, held captive by the weather, he was considering trying his luck with her. He had grown lazy over the years, women tended to fall into his hands without much effort on his part. Perhaps it was time to take out his seduction skills and dust them off.

Chapter Three

CATHERINE DREW UP her stockings and fastened them with a ribbon just above her knee. Despite the fire in the hearth, the room was chilly, and after her attempted foray outdoors she was eager to get dressed. Maggie had informed her that breakfast was being served downstairs in a private parlor. Her maid's visit to the stables had been well spent, and she was able to share with her mistress that there were several guests taking shelter at the inn.

Maggie ticked them off on imaginary fingers as she knelt to slide on Catherine's slippers. "You, Viscount Albury, Mr. and Mrs. Fotheringham and their child, Mr. Querol and his niece."

"Who was the man you were gossiping with?" Catherine had briefly seen the neatly-dressed man with the battered face before he left to seek out his master.

"That's Dodds," she said, with a grin. "A bit of a head turner, isn't he?"

Catherine wasn't sure that was the right description for a man with a broken nose, but perhaps he had hidden depths. Maggie obviously preferred Dodds to other options—she had forsaken the groom who had first caught her eye.

"He's Albury's man," Maggie went on. "The other guests don't have the luxury of help, so they'll be relying on the staff at the inn. And I think the inn is shorthanded because the weather has kept some of them at home."

"It may only be a short stay," Catherine said bracingly, although she didn't really believe it. Last night when they had sought shelter at The White Rose from the howling winds and thick sheets of snow, it had felt as though they would be buried alive. The elements had quietened now, but the damage had already been done.

Maggie shot her a sideways look. "Viscount Albury is a fine-looking fellow. Have you met him? In London I mean."

Catherine smoothed down her skirts. "I've met him. In fact, Winstanton warned me against him."

Maggie thought that was funny. "Probably jealous. Albury's the sort of man who knows what he's doing when it comes to the ladies. They're lining up for a night in his bed. At least that's what Dodds told me."

Catherine said nothing. She was remembering the way the viscount's strikingly pale blue eyes had plotted her curves and the feel of his large hands pressed to her nearly naked skin. The sensations he had stirred up hadn't gone away, and she wanted to squeeze her thighs together to ease the ache inside.

"You deserve a bit of fun," Maggie said, as she arranged a cashmere shawl about Catherine's shoulders. She turned her mistress toward the speckled mirror. "There, how could he resist?"

Catherine stared back at herself. Her looks had been her fortune when she was nineteen and her mother brought her three daughters to London to tempt wealthy gentlemen into marriage. They had succeeded beyond their wildest expectations. Catherine had married the Duke of Winstanton, which was considered an astounding accomplishment for a young, penniless woman of little importance. Astounding, it might have been, but apart from her son, the marriage had brought her no happiness, no joy, and certainly no pleasure.

"Do you think he'd be interested?" Her stomach felt full of

butterflies.

Maggie took her by the shoulders and stared into her reflection's eyes. "Of course he would! Trapped here in the middle of nowhere, you'll be the perfect distraction. Flirt with him. A man like that is always ready for a flirtation. Enjoy yourself . . . *for once*," she added under her breath.

That was always Maggie's refrain: *Enjoy yourself.* And her maid had done so on numerous occasions. She did not believe in waiting for an invitation to a lover's bed. *What's the point of dilly-dallying? Speak up, tell him what you want, or it will never happen.*

"This is the chance you've been waiting for," she went on now. "Albury is perfect for a night or two of debauchery. And once you realize how uncomplicated it can be, you can look around for someone more permanent. Your new footman at Winstanton, for instance, he's a handsome devil."

No, thank you. Maggie had probably already sampled him. But she was right when she said Albury looked like he knew what he was doing when it came to bed sport. She was a widow and he was a bachelor, and they would be hurting no one. Who was there to know or care? She could travel on to her estate and never see him again, and if she did happen to cross his path, she could smile enigmatically and walk on. One thing she had learned from her sister Sophia—in the polite world, if one was discreet, one could do as one pleased behind closed doors.

A night in Albury's arms, his soft lips against hers, and his tall, strong body pressing her down into the mattress. She had dreamed of it for so long, she could not bear to let this opportunity pass her by simply because she was a little bit anxious.

"I'll do it." She smiled gamely at Maggie, and her maid grinned back.

Then Maggie's grin faded and her grey eyes were suddenly serious. "Although, it would be a mistake to believe yourself in love with him, because he will never love you. He is the sort who chooses a lady, beds her, and then walks away."

Catherine knew her maid thought her too soft-hearted, but

she wasn't a fool. It was obvious Albury wasn't the sort of man any woman should fall in love with.

"There is no fear of me doing that," she said with complete confidence.

Satisfied with her appearance, Catherine went downstairs to the private parlor. As she lingered outside the door, the memory of the viscount's warm hands on her returned in full force, and with it the fire in his eyes as he mapped her body through the thin nightdress. Her skin tingled, and hot blood coursed through her veins. It was a reminder that despite her solitary existence she was a young woman, one who longed for the sort of gratification others took for granted. Maggie was right, she needed to speak up and tell Albury exactly what she wanted.

She opened the door.

The room was warm and a little stuffy. A fire roared in the fireplace and the small panes in the window were fogged from the cold air outside while the head of an animal with antlers overlooked the scene from its position above the mantle. The parlor consisted of one large rectangular table and a smaller round one, and the former was already occupied with guests. It appeared that everyone wanted to partake of a hearty breakfast despite having nowhere to go.

A loud, overbearing voice drew her attention to a red-faced, frowning man who was complaining to a serving maid and pointing at his plate, while the buxom younger woman beside him stared at her lap in what could have been embarrassment. *Or*, Catherine thought, noting the curl of her lips, *amusement*. A couple with a child sat conversing quietly over their meal. The child, a boy, had a bored droop to his mouth but when he saw Catherine enter the room, he perked up and gave her a grin.

He reminded her painfully of Jack as she smiled back, at the same time asking herself: Where was Albury? Another glance about the parlor showed her that she had been right the first time—Albury wasn't here. Disappointment washed over her, but she lifted her chin and refused to let it sway her. Now she had made up her mind, she wanted to act immediately.

As Catherine made her way into the room, the others introduced themselves. The complaining gentleman and his younger companion were Mr. Querol and Anthea Querol, his niece, traveling to Scotland. Although Catherine had her doubts. There was something arch about Miss Querol's smile, and something nervous about the way her uncle cleared his throat and tucked his napkin into the top of his waistcoat when he introduced her.

The family of three were the Fotheringhams, and their son's name was Benny. "Benjamin actually," he said importantly. "Only my family and friends call me Benny. You can, too, if you like."

"Benny," whispered his mother, with an anxious glance at Catherine.

"It would be my privilege to call you Benny," she assured him gravely. "I have a son, too, not much older than you, and his name is Alfred Algernon Jonathon, but we call him Jack."

"Is he here?" Benny looked about hopefully. "We could make a snowman together."

"No, he's not," Catherine tried to keep her smile. "He's at home."

There wasn't time for more. The serving maid was quick to direct her to the smaller table, and poured her a cup of coffee, placing the cream close by. She promised that Catherine's meal would be with her directly but had barely left the room when the door opened again and a tall fair-haired gentleman stood surveying the room.

Sebastian, Viscount Albury, had changed from his outdoor clothes into a brown jacket over a white shirt, the necktie casually knotted about his throat. Fawn pantaloons and boots polished to a mirror shine completed his outfit. He wore his fashionable clothing well, and he had a comfortable charm that, despite his title and breeding, allowed him to fit into any situation with ease.

Albury was looking about him in much the same way Catherine had done, and when his gaze found her, those blue eyes narrowed with satisfaction. With nods and smiles to the other guests, he made his way unhesitatingly to her side.

"So *you* are the duchess everyone is whispering about?" he said in a low, teasing voice, as he sat down. He had shaved, the stubble she had noticed earlier was gone, and his skin was smooth. Catherine wanted to nuzzle against him like a cat.

Those butterflies in her stomach were now flitting about in other parts of her body. She smiled as she pretended to busy herself arranging the napkin on her lap. "I don't know why everyone is whispering about me. But yes, I am the Dowager Duchess of Winstanton."

"We *have* met."

She looked up with pleased surprise. "You remembered?"

"You were about to be married to Winstanton. I thought it an unfortunate choice." There was a pinch between his fair brows.

Catherine didn't know what to say. She tried a smile, but his eyes were cataloguing her features. She was used to being stared at, but there was something about Albury's focus that was different. His gaze remained on her lips for longer than was polite before his eyes returned to hers with heat shimmering in their depths.

Her voice had a breathless quality, as if there wasn't enough air in the room. "We should not speak ill of the dead."

"My condolences, although Winstanton must have been of quite an advanced age." He cocked an eyebrow.

Was he implying something about the disparity in their ages? He looked innocent enough, but she felt a prickle at the back of her neck. He probably thought her a fortune hunter, and he would be right. Her mother had set her daughters before the gentlemen of the *ton* like sweets in a confectioner's shop.

"You are traveling to Winstanton?" he said, when she did not speak. He was still watching her, this time like a puzzle he was trying to solve. "It is not far from my father's estate, but they were never friends. The duke was not a gregarious man."

"He was a scholar. A collector." And Catherine had been his

prize exhibit in that grim, walled fortress.

"I remember. I would have thought you'd return to live in London as quickly as possible now you are a widow. Surely there is nothing to keep you at Winstanton?" His hand was resting on the table, his long fingers half curled, one of them tapping upon the surface.

Catherine wasn't about to tell him the details of her husband's will. "There are reasons why I must remain there."

"It seems cruel to keep a beautiful woman locked away like that. I thought so when we first met, and I still do. It must be a lonely life. Do you not crave . . . company?"

He had moved closer to her, keeping their conversation private, and Catherine could see the question in his eyes. This was the moment. She took a steadying breath.

But before she could speak, the servant returned with their meals. Flustered, she agreed to the addition of toast, and then there was the business of buttering it, and pouring tea for Albury and more coffee for her.

Finally, the girl left them alone again but perhaps Catherine's moment had passed, because when Albury next spoke it was to offer mere polite chitchat.

"You have sisters. I am acquainted with one of them. Sophia."

Catherine swallowed her impatience and made herself smile. "Everyone who is anyone in London knows Sophia."

"And you have another sister?"

"Ellis. She is the youngest."

He had remembered the full story now—she could see it in the speculative look he sent her—and maybe he no longer wanted to discuss her craving for company. "And the three of you are all duchesses?" His mouth gave a wry twist. *Fortune hunters, mercenaries, opportunists, adventuresses, grubbers* . . . They were just some of the names they had been called.

"Once I married the duke, our mother decided my two sisters must also marry dukes."

"A determined woman. Did you have no say in this?"

Catherine didn't want to talk about the past. At the time it had seemed like a dream for the poor girl she had been, until it became a nightmare. Some people found the thought titillating—a young girl and a much older husband—and if Albury was one of them, then perhaps she should rethink her plan.

"I have offended you," he said, his deep voice apologetic. "It was not my intention."

Her voice was cool. "I am not offended."

"I don't care who you married, Catherine, and I am selfish enough to be pleased about your widowed state." The mischievous twist to his mouth was all the warning she had. "Perhaps you know of my reputation? I would think a beautiful woman, locked away in that hideous castle, might want to take advantage of my expertise."

Startled, hopeful, her eyes met his. There was understanding in them rather than derision. Catherine licked suddenly dry lips, and his pupils flared. Desire. Oh yes, Albury wanted her.

"You are right," she began, her voice too low to be heard by anyone but him. Her heart was beating furiously. "I am in dire need of your . . . expertise, Viscount. Can we discuss this further? The two of us. Alone."

He studied her in silence and then he smiled, his teeth white and straight. "I would very much like that, Duchess." He leaned in closer, and his breath tickled her ear. She could smell him, citrus pomade and clean male. *If I turn now I could brush my lips against his.* Catherine was shocked at how difficult it was to refrain, despite knowing the parlor was full of people. "An intimate interlude before we resume our journeys."

A moment later he was cutting into his meal.

"Eat up, Duchess. You will need your strength."

Chapter Four

SEBASTIAN HAD REMEMBERED the story about the three duchesses. They had begun as three beautiful but poor girls from a village no one had heard of, brought to London by their ambitious mother. There had been some relative with connections, one who was willing to help place the girls before the most eligible gentlemen.

It had caused a riot. Eligible—and ineligible—gentlemen had scrambled for the sisters' attentions, but the mother had been very specific in her requirements. She had wanted dukes for her daughters, and dukes she had secured.

Winstanton had been old even then, but that hadn't stopped Catherine marrying him. There had been gossip, but Seb had been on the fringes of the whole thing, twenty-one years old and with no plans to find a wife. There were too many pretty women arrayed before him, and too many opportunities to indulge himself in the pleasures of the flesh. He'd lost himself in all London had to offer, filling his mind with so many sights and sounds that there was no room for the past that haunted him.

These days, he knew Catherine's sister, Sophia, quite well. Their paths crossed often enough in London. She made him think of a cut gemstone. Beautiful but hard and cold, and with her secrets well hidden behind the sparkly surface. Unlike Catherine, who sat beside him now, who seemed . . . softer somehow. She had the same cool restraint as her sister, but there was a tranquillity to her. Seb supposed Catherine might be on the hunt for her next husband rather than a few sweaty hours in his bed, but if she was . . . well, that husband would not be Sebastian, the most confirmed bachelor in England.

She *was* beautiful, though—his sideways glance showed him her creamy skin, the perfect curve of her cheek, and the way her long dark lashes lay upon it. Desire stirred and his cock filled. Hell, it was already sitting up and taking notice. The memory of her half-naked body made him want to groan aloud.

I am in dire need of your expertise.

He couldn't be mistaking her meaning, could he? No, this was a game he was too well versed in to be mistaken. She wanted him as much as he wanted her. He glanced at her again and found she was looking at him. Those liquescent dark eyes searched his, a little uncertain, and then dropped to his mouth.

Oh, yes, Seb knew that look. He curved his lips into a lazy smile, and her gaze jumped back to his eyes and widened. She was a novice when it came to the art of seduction, and right now she seemed to be both anxious and attracted to him in equal measure. Well, it was his job to persuade her that spending some time with him, naked, was to both their advantages.

Just then the piping voice of a child cut through the clink of cutlery and the low murmur of voices. "Mama, *why* can't we leave now?"

The family were seated behind him at the larger table, but he could hear them perfectly. "Because of the snow," the father replied patiently, despite it being a question he had probably heard several times already that morning. "It is too deep on the roads, and therefore it is unsafe to drive. We might go the wrong way, or tip into a ditch. Then what would we do, Benny?"

"We could walk!"

The couple laughed in fond delight.

Instinctively Sebastian smiled too, only to find those dark

eyes still watching him. She appeared to be trying to understand him better, and he wasn't sure he liked that. What was there to understand? They would fuck and then go their separate ways. And yet . . . he supposed he should make the effort at polite conversation.

"Do you have children?" he asked, buttering a slice of toast.

She looked down at her plate. "I have a son." When she met his eyes again there was pain in them. Something about her son did not make her happy.

"And do you have children?" she asked, obviously keen to move the subject away from herself. The next moment her cheeks flushed in mortification. "I'm so sorry, that was an inappropriate question. You are a bachelor, are you not?"

"Yes, I am single, and no, I don't have children." Albury, the house and the estate, would finish with him. He heard again his father's voice during that last, bitter argument.

"You will inherit Albury when I am dead, but I do not want to see you ever again."

"My mother—"

"Your mother is dead and you killed her. I warned you never to let her drive the gig, but you didn't listen to me. I want you to leave this house and never return, do you understand? I wish to God it was you who'd died and not her."

Sebastian cleared his throat. He was weary of mulling over the past. What he needed was a distraction, and that distraction was seated right beside him. Her hands rested in her lap beneath the table, and he could see her fingers twisting in the napkin. He reached to cover them, his much larger hand closing over her cool, agitated fingers. She startled and then stilled.

"We have an assignation. Yes or no?" Seb whispered. It was always best to be perfectly clear.

She looked about the room, and once she was certain they were not being observed, she turned to him. "Yes," she whispered.

Her gaze dropped, her lashes sweeping down to brush her

pale skin. Oh God, were they freckles? There was a light dusting of them across the bridge of her nose. Why had he not noticed them before? Sebastian's cock swelled embarrassingly—he had a particular weakness for women with freckles.

Catherine swallowed, the tip of her tongue licking over her lips, and Sebastian's desire increased another notch.

"My room is the first one at the top of the stairs," he said quietly, and rose to his feet. A quick glance assured him that no one else had noticed their exchange—not that it mattered to him, but he suspected Catherine would not like it. The parents were smiling at their child, and the older man and his niece seemed to be in the middle of an argument.

"Now?" she gasped. "But . . . it's daylight."

Sebastian grinned. She was adorable. "So it is, Duchess." He gave her one last, meaningful look and left the room.

Dodds was upstairs, folding his clothing. He frowned as he noticed a loose button. "It's been snowing again," he grumbled to Seb. "No sign of it clearing either. We're stuck here for the foreseeable future."

"You should look at this as a chance to broaden your horizons. The world doesn't begin and end with the City of London."

Dodds was a Londoner through and through and always let his master know it. "I've seen more snow since we left Mayfair than I've seen before in my whole life," he grumbled.

"May I suggest you find that pretty maid you were talking about and share your complaints with her? I am about to have company."

Dodds stared and then grinned. "The devil you are! All right, I'm going." He was out of the door in a flash, and Seb huffed a laugh. He and his manservant had been together for a very long time. They had met one night when young Seb, the worse for drink, had tried to enter a club, and Dodds, at the door, had told him to go home and sleep it off. Seb had not been long in the capitol then and was probably in danger of overdoing it. They began to talk, and found they had a lot in common. Dodds had also been thrown out of home by his father and been forced to make his own way—he'd had barely two shillings to rub together before he took to the boxing circuit. When Seb went back the next day and offered him a job, he took it, and now Seb could not imagine life without him.

With Dodds gone there was nothing to do but wait, and Seb lacked patience. Restlessly, he took the two steps necessary to reach the window, drawn despite himself by the bleak forest with slivers of icicles adorning the bare branches. Again, it reminded him of Albury House. He dreaded walking through that door and back into his past. For twelve years it had been as if he did not exist. As if he had ceased to be. Exiled to London by a father who could not forgive him.

The earl could not know that his son's life in London, once so exciting, had grown stale and tedious. The endless round of pleasures no longer called to him and hadn't for some time. When he found his funds dwindling, and having sworn to never ask his father for anything ever, he began to invest in various businesses and found he had a talent for choosing the successful ones. He now had a tidy sum tucked away in his bank account.

He had no plans to marry. He had seen what happened when one lost the person one loved. He had felt the remorse and regret, had his heart torn apart, and been forced to live far away from his home and what remained of his family. He never wanted to inflict that pain on someone else.

And if his father died? He had yet to decide what he would do then. He tried to imagine taking over the estate, filling his time with farming and ledgers. He had been brought up to be the heir, and with a bit of effort he could probably remember those lessons his father had instilled in him. Back when he still loved him. Before he abandoned him. London society would laugh at the idea of Sebastian turning his back on his carefree existence to become a country gentleman, but they did not know him. Very few people did know the man behind the veneer that was Seb's way of protecting himself against further hurt.

Just as his thoughts began to grow too gloomy, there was a tap on the door, and his spirits lifted. A beautiful woman was offering him a distraction, and Sebastian was more than eager to accept. Pleasure was a great diversion. At least for an hour or two.

Chapter Five

CATHERINE LIFTED HER hand to the door. Had she waited long enough? Did she seem too eager? Her heart was beating so wildly it was making her feel a little giddy. She told herself that she didn't have to be here, she could say no or change her mind, and probably he would not care. But she didn't want to say no, and she didn't want to change her mind. She wanted to be with this man, she wanted to discover the pleasures she had been missing, and if she stepped away now then she might never have another chance.

She knocked and heard steps moving toward her before the door opened.

Albury had taken off his jacket. His shoulders looked broader in his white shirt, and the long line of his muscled legs was lovingly embraced by skintight pantaloons. His shirt ballooned out over his waistband but beneath it she could see the buttoned flap and the swell of his manhood. Realizing she was staring, she quickly lifted her gaze to his.

He was smiling, but his expression was quizzical.

"We are in agreement then?" he said quietly. "While we are here, we will spend our time in pleasure, but once the road is clear, we will go our separate ways."

"Yes. I agree." She sounded impatient. Didn't he believe her?

To further persuade him she put her hand up and rested it lightly in the center of his chest. His skin was warm through the fine linen, and she could feel the hard curve of bone and muscle moving with each breath. Before she could explore further, he took her hand in his and led her into his room, closing the door behind them.

His room was much like hers, but Catherine wasn't interested in that. It was the man before her who held her attention. He was still holding her hand, his thumb brushing over her palm. He drew her closer. She could see a pulse beating in the hollow of his throat and she needed to press her face to it. Because he was taller, she had to stand up on her tiptoes before she was able to nuzzle against him and let the clean scent of his skin fill her senses.

She had never explored a man's body before, but now she wanted to see every part of him, run her hands over him, everywhere. She rested her cheek beneath the jut of his jaw, on his smoothly shaven skin, and at the same time she felt him taking down her hair. Slowly, pin by pin, until he could run his fingers through the thick tresses. A tug on those tresses lifted her face to his.

She gazed up at him, lost in the fire in his eyes, and then his mouth was on hers.

He licked across her lips and, when she opened them, slid his tongue inside. It was shocking to her, the intensity of feeling, the rush of sensation. Catherine had never been kissed like this before. So completely, so thoroughly. She was panting when he drew away, her skin hot and tingling, her breasts tight and aching.

"Oh, yes," he said, his voice deeper and full of satisfaction. "You taste delicious." He smiled down at her and she felt her bones melt.

Eagerly, wanting to lose herself again in this new, heady delight, she stretched up for more kisses. She felt his hands fumble with the back of her gown, where there were hooks that held it together. With a groan of frustration he turned her about and set to work again. As he bent closer his warm breath on her nape made her shiver in delight, and he gave a soft laugh. He pressed his lips to her skin, one for each hook undone, until her bodice loosened and began to slip over her shoulders.

Large, warm hands slid beneath the cloth and cupped her breasts over her satiny chemise, and suddenly all of Catherine's senses were centered there.

With a soft moan she leaned back into him. There was an ache between her thighs, as if she was readying herself for him. An ache her husband had never accomplished, let alone satisfied. He had never even tried to bring her the pleasure she knew was possible. The bodice of her gown was at her waist now, and Albury pushed her chemise down to join it, baring her completely to his touch and his gaze, as he turned her back around.

No man had ever seen her naked before, apart from the one who had purchased her to complete his collection. That first night of their marriage he had told her to strip and then admired her from a distance. She had felt frightened and vulnerable, and just for a moment those feelings rose up again. But Albury's gaze was so different. She could tell she wasn't an object to him, to be looked upon with the cool gaze of a curator. She was a flesh and blood woman, and he did not try to hide his craving for her.

He groaned, reaching to brush his fingertip gently over a nipple, then rolling it gently between his fingers. Watching as it tightened and peaked.

"Oh!" She gave a gasp of surprise and wonder that such a light touch could send her senses spinning.

He did it again, feeding on her reactions. Then slowly he walked her backward to his bed until she sat down. Catherine wondered if he would push her flat, take her with raw urgency, but instead he stood before her and without haste began to unfasten the ties of his shirt. Her gaze was riveted to him and his slow, sensuous movements. He was teasing her, she realized, as he lazily lifted the garment up over his body, disclosing all that warm skin and hard muscle. A line of hair ran down from the thicker patch on his chest, darker than the hair on his head, and vanished beneath the waist of his pantaloons. When he tugged his shirt off over his head, his muscles bunched and stretched, like some big, barely-tamed jungle animal. Her gaze ran over him, admiring, desiring, and found the now obvious bulge of his cock. If she had ever doubted that his hunger for her was as strong as hers for him, then here was the proof.

Catherine clutched her hands together as she looked up and met his gaze. She desperately wanted to touch him, but the duke had taught her that touching was forbidden. And yet her need to do so must have been obvious to Albury, because he took a step closer, so that he was within easy reach, and widened his stance.

"Unbutton me," he said in a gravelly voice. "Take me out."

She caught her breath and didn't move.

"Unbutton me, *Your Grace*," he teased, as though the use of her title could persuade her to obey him.

She needed no such persuasion. Her fingers were already at the flap of his pants, fumbling only a bit as she opened the buttons before she reached inside. Her hand closed around the hot, hard heat of him, and his head fell back on a deep groan.

"Yes, like that," he rasped. His thighs were shaking. That her inexperienced touch could do this to such a man was a revelation to her. Any remaining doubts fled, and eagerly she pushed down his breeches, to uncover him completely. His cock was long and thick, with the flushed skin soft over rigid flesh. His seed was already leaking from the tip and on impulse she ran her tongue around him, closing her eyes as she savoured the unfamiliar salty taste.

He muttered a profanity and reached for her, tangling his hands in her hair. "Suck me," he groaned. "I need . . . I need . . ."

She eyed him a moment, chewing in her lip. It was all very well to give her such an instruction, but his shaft was far bigger than the only other one she had ever seen. Not that she had sucked on the duke's member, nor had he wanted her to. But this was different, and she was not averse to doing her utmost. She leaned forward and once again used her tongue before her mouth closed over the tip. She sucked and his knees shook.

"Fuck."

His reaction, the profanity, made her look up, and she found he was observing her from beneath his lashes, a flush on his cheeks, and the lines of his face more finely drawn. "You are my every lustful dream," he admitted in a strained voice, before he took a step back, allowing his cock to fall from her lips. "If we had more time I would like to spill in your mouth, but right now I would much rather be inside you. It is what I've wanted since I walked into the inn and you fell into my arms."

Was that only a few hours ago?

"May I call you Catherine?" he asked, as he tugged off his boots and tossed the remainder of his clothes carelessly about. The polite question in such circumstances made her smile.

"You may. Should I call you—"

"Sebastian," he said, kneeling before her.

His gaze was on her breasts, and he couldn't seem to help himself as he leaned forward to kiss and suckle at the pink points. She clutched at his short and springy hair, and once again the scent of his citrus pomade filled her senses. The ache between her thighs had intensified to the point where she wondered whether she might burst. The need increased with each lathe of his tongue on her sensitive skin.

When he stopped, she murmured in protest, but he was unpeeling her from her gown and chemise, impatiently tossing both onto the growing pile. Only her stockings remained now, neatly tied above her knees. His gaze wandered up her thighs, to the dark wedge of hair, as he untied the bows, removing first one and then the other.

"You are very beautiful," he said.

She shook her head a little wildly. "No, don't say that."

Startled, his gaze jumped to hers. "Surely you know it is the truth? You *are* beautiful." His eyes narrowed. "Did Winstanton not tell you so, the old goat?"

Catherine swallowed, because those memories were repugnant.

"Tell me," Seb insisted, staring back at her. There was a glint of anger in his eyes on her behalf, as if he genuinely cared. It convinced her to speak.

"Yes, he did tell me I was beautiful. In the early days, he had me stand before him at bedtime, and he would examine every inch of me. With his eyes. He said he wanted to be sure I was still perfect. And then he would spill in his hand so as not to despoil me."

Sebastian listened to her in shocked silence. "You cannot be a virgin," he growled. "You said you have a son."

Catherine sighed. "He took me, sometimes, when he couldn't help himself. But he was always angry afterward, claiming it was my fault his self-control had failed him."

Winstanton had claimed it would be sacrilege to use her so basely. Only rarely did he poke and prod between her legs, grunting and groaning. And he always blamed her afterward. And when she had fallen pregnant with their son, he had loathed the sight of her. He called her swollen body an abomination, and after Jack was born, he had insisted on inspecting her once again, to be sure she was still perfect. Catherine had hoped for a lingering mark or two, something to keep him away from her, but apart from her swollen breasts there had been nothing to show she was now a mother.

"Catherine."

Sebastian seemed to read the unhappy emotions crossing her face as she sat naked before him. Would he reject her now? Would he not want to make love to a woman with such a sordid tale to tell?

But he was speaking again, in a low urgent voice, and it was a moment before she grasped what he was saying. "Looking is all well and good, but I want to kiss every inch of you. I want to put my mark upon you, Catherine. I want you to feel me inside you. And even when I am gone, I want my seed to trickle down your thighs so that you will remember it was me who put it there."

She wasn't shocked. She was elated. He did not see her as cool and untouchable, something to admire behind a glass door in a trophy case.

"Yes, yes!" she gasped. "Touch me. Make me *feel* you."

He began to trace her curves with hands and tongue, and it was so good. She had never been fragile. She was a woman who needed to be held and loved, and finally she had found a man who was happy to show her all that she had been missing. She was going to rejoice in every moment of it.

Chapter Six

HE WANTED TO lick every inch of her creamy skin and suckle on her pert breasts with those oh-so-enticingly pink tips. The dark hair at the juncture of her thighs, too, he wanted his tongue there. His fingers. His cock. He wanted to claim her and make her his in the most fundamental of ways.

Sebastian was a lover who knew what he wanted, but he never expected to own the woman he held in his arms. He would move on to other lovers and so would she. But *this* woman . . . she was bringing out an element of his personality he had never experienced before: The selfish desire to keep her entirely to himself. But wasn't that what her late husband had done?

He had seen the expression on her face when she spoke of her marriage, and it was enough to cool even his passion. For a moment anyway. To be gazed at and admired and rarely touched, and then blamed for that touch—it was horrifying to a man who relished the earthy sounds and smells and sensations of intercourse. That she had been denied those basic pleasures for so long made him all the more determined to introduce her to them now.

He wanted to show her how desirable she was, and how only a fool like Winstanton would stand at a distance and stare at her while he brought himself off.

Seb slid his hands beneath her, cupping the globes of her bottom and squeezing that delectable flesh, before he maneuvered her farther back onto his bed. Obediently she lay there, watching him, but her body was a little tense. To relax her, he kissed her, stroking her tongue with his, as he spread himself out above her. She was smaller than him, and more delicate, but he dismissed the idea that she was breakable as he pressed his body lightly along her length, his knees and elbows taking most of his weight. Her scent was addictive, and he nuzzled against her throat, sucking and licking in the hollows and crevices.

The tips of her breasts were pressed to his chest, and she must have enjoyed the sensation because she rubbed against him. He nudged her thighs apart with one of his, and reached down to finger her lower lips, discovering her wet with the essence of her desire. It was the proof that she wanted him just as much as he wanted her, and he didn't hesitate to push one finger gently inside her, while his thumb stroked the bud already swollen and eager for his touch.

She let out a surprised cry, hips rising, while she arched back her head.

"Yes?" He bent again to her throat to taste her skin, while he circled his thumb with more resolve. She was going to come if he kept up his attentions—he knew the signs. Her legs were tangling with his as she tried desperately to get closer, and he felt her soft, quick breaths against his shoulder as she answered him in murmurs and moans.

"Please," she managed, reaching down to place his cock where she wanted it.

He was so hard he ached, and it was a relief to push himself inside her. *Slowly*, he reminded himself. She was not an experienced lover, and he didn't want to rush her or hurt her. He wanted her enjoyment to be as great as his. He withdrew, brushing against her most sensitive part, and then pushed inside again. Deeper now. She was hot and tight, and he thought at this moment he could die happy. He was fully inside her now, so deep that his body felt a part of hers. Blindly, he kissed her, aware of nothing but the physical sensation, and the quickening spiral of pleasure.

Her hands were clutching at the bunched muscles of his buttocks, feeling him move as he rocked against her. With a gasp, her mouth searched for his, as if he were the only thing keeping her tethered to the bed.

Once again he reached down to stroke between her legs, withdrawing almost all the way out of her body, before pushing in again, rocking against her in this most ancient and fundamental of ways.

"What do you need?" he asked, between kisses.

"You," she said. "I want you."

She was close to her climax, and even as he thought it, her body tensed, and then she cried out so loudly he muffled the sound against his lips. He moved quickly now, eager to join her, as the flood of feeling grew and grew. He heard her cry out again as he soared upward.

The wave of pleasure that engulfed him was almost too much to bear. With his face pressed into the pillow beside hers, he lay gasping and shuddering, aware of her body boneless in his arms. For a moment he couldn't speak, could only lay in her warm grasp, as the world slowly righted itself.

It was an effort to roll over, but he knew he was too heavy for her. With a grunt he settled beside her, his shoulder brushing against hers, and finally turned his head to look at her. Her eyes were closed, but at his movement, her dark lashes fluttered and lifted and she blinked, staring up at the ceiling. She looked debauched, the marks of his mouth and hands on her fair skin, her hair a tangled mess, and her breasts heaving with each breath. But to him she was more beautiful like this than as that perfect woman who had first stepped inside his room.

Voices. He recognized that of the Fotheringham child, and then his parents, as they made their way back to their room. Laughter drifted from elsewhere in the inn, and he thought he heard Dodds, but it was all far away. Like a memory or a dream.

Could this be the most intense sexual experience he had ever had?

Realizing he was watching her, Catherine reached to cover herself, only to change her mind and let her hands fall back. Goosebumps erupted across her skin.

"You are cold," he said, and began to draw the covers over her. A glance at the fireplace showed that the fire was now only an insipid glow. He rose and went to place more wood upon the coals, squatting as he used the poker to urge them into life.

When he looked back to the bed she was sitting up, watching him, one hand holding the covers to her breasts while her dark hair tumbled about her. He stood up, and her gaze raked over him, and then again, more slowly, as if she was implanting the memory of him in her mind.

All that attention went right to his cock. He was already moving back to the bed, ready for another round, when there was a knock on the door.

"Sir?" It was a woman's voice, one of the maids. "Can I tidy your room?"

"No," he said sharply and impatiently, "you cannot." Then, remembering himself, "Not right now, thank you."

Her steps faded away as Seb climbed onto the bed and reached for Catherine, his fingers tangling in her hair as he cupped the back of her head. He pinned her there and began to kiss her, slowly at first, exploring her lips and then using his tongue to take her mouth as thoroughly as he had just taken her body. She clung to him, her nails making little half-moons in the skin of his shoulders.

Seb smiled. She was as insatiable for him as he was for her. And that was good, because he meant to have her as often as time and stamina would allow before the road was cleared and they went their separate ways.

Chapter Seven

CATHERINE LAY, HER body pleasantly aching, aware that she was not in her own room. Or in her own bed. Through the single window she could see snow falling outside and collecting on the window ledge. It seemed the weather was still holding them hostage, and suddenly she was glad of it. Ridiculously glad.

She sat up, tucking her hair out of the way, and looked down at the man sleeping beside her. His fair lashes covered those strikingly pale blue eyes, and his full mouth was slightly open, soft breaths huffing in and out. His lips had been so soft, and when he had smiled she had felt that smile against her own. There was a beard beginning to sprout on his cheeks and jaw, the stubble a darker shade than his hair.

She wanted to run her fingers over it. She wanted . . . well, she wanted to do it all over again.

While he slept he had thrown off the covers, and now he lay on his back, completely naked to her gaze. In her ignorance she had believed she knew what a man looked like, that they were all the same, but *this* man . . . so handsome, so well made, she could gaze at him for hours. Long, muscled legs and narrow hips, his chest broader, and his shoulders broader still. She contemplated the flesh between his legs, lying soft against his thigh. The memory of his expertise, the way he had played her body like an instrument, knowing exactly how to extract the most bliss from it, made her cheeks warm.

She had never been loved like that. She had never thought physical pleasure could be so all consuming unless it was accompanied by strong emotion. *Love.* But she did not love Sebastian, and he did not love her, although the attraction between them seemed incredibly strong. Potent. When he had brought her to her climax she had hardly known where she was. A weightless creature, soaring into the sky, while the world vanished beneath her. It had been unlike even her most vivid imaginings.

Was that just her lack of experience, or was it this man? She didn't want it to be the latter because their arrangement was meant to be temporary. When they parted she would remember him, but she did not want to yearn for him. She wanted to smile at her memories, find pleasure in them, and not ache with the sorrow of loss.

Perhaps Maggie was right, and she should seek out the new footman. But the idea repulsed her. She didn't want to think about another man, not while Sebastian lay beside her. It felt . . . wrong. She simply wanted to luxuriate in his company in the short time remaining to them.

When she was young, there had been little time for leisure. Her father had worked long hours as the curate in their parish where the vicar was often absent. Her mother was his helpmate, and his daughters loved his kind and gentle ways. When he died suddenly, crushed when his horse fell and rolled on him, they lost their father and husband, but also their provider. Poverty dug its claws into them, and although the people of the parish tried to help, it was not enough. That was the moment when Ellen Mallory had decided to take advantage of her three daughters' extraordinary good looks, and a cousin's invitation, and move them all to London.

"So many opportunities, girls!" she had declared, her eyes shining with hope and ambition. "You will thank me for this chance!"

Catherine agreed that being desperately poor was not something anyone would want, but to be married to a man old enough to be her grandfather just for his coronet . . .?

There was a soft tap on the door. Catherine, startled out of her memories, wondered if Sebastian would wake, but he barely stirred. She rose, collecting her clothing and slipping on her gown over her naked body. She was already at the door when Maggie's whisper reached her.

"My lady? Are you there?"

Catherine opened the door a crack.

Maggie grinned at her. "I didn't want to disturb you if you were busy," she said innocently. "Although it seemed awfully quiet in there."

"I . . . we were sleeping," she replied as she went into the hallway and shut the door quietly behind her, knowing her cheeks were pink.

Maggie didn't seem to feel the same embarrassment. "There's hot water, if you want to bathe," she said, walking close beside Catherine as they made their way back to her room. "I've had Dodds carrying the buckets up here."

"Dodds? Oh, the viscount's manservant."

"He has nothing to do while his master is *busy*, so I set him to work."

She looked so pleased with herself that Catherine laughed. It was a happy sound, and Maggie noticed. "I heard them saying downstairs that the road is not looking like it will be open for at least another day," she said, with another broad grin.

More time with Sebastian. More hours of sensual pleasure. She hugged the thought to herself. And she would still be home in time for Jack's birthday.

In her room there was a steaming hot bath waiting for her, just as Maggie had promised. "If you weren't needing it, I would have used it myself," her servant said cheekily.

"Thank you," Catherine whispered, clasping Maggie's hand. "It is just what I need."

Maggie swished some scent into the water while Catherine undressed again. She gave her mistress a sly glance. "Well? You haven't said whether it was as good as I am thinking? Don't tell me a fine-looking specimen like Albury didn't know where to put his—"

Catherine interrupted with a frown. "It was very good, Maggie, and he was a master of—of seduction. Although I was more than ready to be seduced." She laughed at herself, pressing her hands to her hot cheeks. "Now ask no more questions for I won't tell you the answers."

"That's hardly fair. I tell you about my conquests." Maggie pouted, as Catherine stepped into the water and sank down with a sigh. She closed her eyes but couldn't rid herself of her smile.

"I did not know . . ." she began, and the words seemed lodged in her throat.

But Maggie understood. "You deserve to be happy," she said. "Enjoy yourself with the viscount."

Catherine felt a little jump of joy inside her. Another night, perhaps, or two? Assuming, that was, Sebastian wanted to repeat their performance. But when she remembered the way his legs had trembled as she sucked him, and his groan as he reached his climax inside her, she had few doubts that he would be as willing as she.

"When Dodds told me his master was an expert in the art of pleasure, I wasn't sure whether or not to believe him." Maggie began to wash Catherine's hair.

Catherine's smile grew. "He is well-versed on the subject."

Maggie gave an unladylike snort. "I'll wager he is."

After she was patted dry and dressed in a plum-colored gown with slippers to match, it was almost time to go down to the parlor. She had missed luncheon, but Maggie assured her it had been very uninspiring. Merely a stopgap before dinner. It was only four o'clock in the afternoon, but folk here in the country ate their dinners early, and if anyone was still ravenous they could partake of supper before bedtime. The meals were probably also meant to give the travelers a sense of structure in their day, when no one quite knew what was happening.

Maggie put the finishing touches on Catherine's hair, coiling it into a simple braid on top of her head, with ringlets about her face to offset the severity of the style.

"I'm sure Albury won't know what to do with himself when he sees you like this," Maggie said, pretending to be serious. "You are always beautiful, but right now . . . you are glowing."

"Nonsense," Catherine retorted. "If I am glowing then it is from the heat of the bath."

"Hmm, if you say so." Maggie's look was arch.

Catherine giggled, shocking herself, because when was the last time she had *giggled*?

They were about to open the door and leave the room, when they heard Mr. Querol and his niece pass by, making their way to the stairs. Once they had passed, Maggie and Catherine stepped out into the passage and followed at a discreet distance. The two Querols were speaking in low, angry voices. The girl, Anthea, certainly looked miffed about something, and she shook off her uncle's hand when he tried to grab hold of her arm. He shot her a sour look in return.

"This was a mistake," he hissed. "I should never have agreed to bring you with me."

"You're telling me," the girl said, and to Catherine's surprise she had a strong Cockney accent very much at odds with her uncle's educated English.

Maggie and Catherine shared a look. When the couple had closed the parlor door behind them, Maggie leaned in close. "If they are uncle and niece, I am the Queen of France."

"They do seem an ill-assorted couple."

Maggie gave her customary snort of laughter. She nodded toward the back of the inn. "I'll be eating in the kitchen with Dodds and the others. Plenty of gossip to be had. I'll see what I can discover about Mr. and Miss Querol."

Catherine stiffened but Maggie was quick to reassure her.

"Not about you. I don't talk about you, my lady, and if any-one else tries to wheedle your secrets from me I'll be quick to shut them up."

Catherine knew she could trust her maid, but she was also wise enough to know there would be gossip about herself and Sebastian. It shouldn't matter to her—it was unlikely she would be returning to The White Rose again—but memories of the whispers when she arrived in London at nineteen lingered. Courage, she told herself, and with a deep breath she pushed her shoulders back and followed the Querols into the parlor.

A quick glance showed her that Sebastian wasn't there. She was disappointed, but the thought of seeing him again after their tryst was also rather unnerving—their time together had rubbed her emotions raw and left her feeling transparent. The other occupants sent smiles and murmurs of greeting her way. The Fotheringhams were at the smaller round table this time, and the Querols were at the end of the large table, nearer the fireplace. This left the other end for Catherine.

A breathless maid had followed her in and now informed everyone that dinner would be delayed as the farmer who was bringing the beef for the roast beef had overturned his cart. There were murmurs of concern and, from Benny, a long one-sided conversation about what that might mean for their dinner. When the maid could get a word in, she assured him that Mr. Rose would be in shortly to discuss the matter, and then she made her escape.

By now Catherine had sat down, and seeing her, Benny called out. "We can't go anywhere because the snow is too deep."

His parents hushed him, but Catherine answered with a smile. "Were you going somewhere in particular, Benny?"

"To my parents," Mrs. Fotheringham replied. "They haven't seen their grandson since he was a babe in arms, so this is a special treat. He's a big boy now."

"I'm four!" Master Fotheringham announced importantly.

"That is a great age," Catherine said seriously. "I'm sure your grandparents will be so pleased to see you."

Mrs. Fotheringham smiled. "What of you, my—my lady?"

Mr. Querol looked up from his tankard of ale. "The proper way of addressing a duchess is 'your grace', Mrs. Fotheringham."

"Oh!" She looked embarrassed. "I didn't—"

"I don't mind in the least," Catherine assured her. "And to answer your question, I am going home to Winstanton to see my son. I have been visiting my mother."

"Why didn't your son go with you? Where did you go?" Benny demanded.

His parents hushed him again, but Catherine loved the way children were so inquisitive. They knew no boundaries in their quest for an answer. Although she would have enjoyed their conversation more if she were not missing Jack so much. "Unfortunately, he couldn't go with me, and my mother lives in London."

"London," the boy said in awe, his eyes alight. "Can *we* go to London next time, Mama?"

Mr. Querol interrupted again. "Nasty place. You don't want to go there, young man. You never know what sort of characters you might meet."

His niece gave him a glare, before she too turned to the child. "It's a wonderful place, my duck, and you will have a wonderful time if you go."

No one seemed to know what to say after that and there was an uncomfortable silence. Catherine was relieved when the door opened again, and this time Sebastian entered the room.

Chapter Eight

S EB HAD AWOKEN to Dodds' gleeful chuckle. "Rise and shine, sir!"

These playful moods of Dodds' didn't happen very often, but when they did Seb found it best to ignore them. As he washed and dressed, Dodds explained how he had carried bucket after bucket of hot water upstairs for the duchess. "I was puffing and panting at the end of it, but Maggie didn't care one jot. She's a high-handed one." But his eyes were shining with affection.

Dodds was just as wedded to being single as Sebastian, so to see him this captivated by a woman was worrying. "We are going our separate ways once the weather clears," he told his manservant, and then wondered just who he was reminding.

"Maggie says the duchess hasn't had a happy time of it," Dodds went on like he hadn't heard. "Old husband, scolding her all the time."

"He was one of the wealthiest men in England, I believe," Seb said dryly. "Hardly a case for pity, Dodds."

Dodds shot him a look. "That was the mother's doing, marrying off her daughters to dukes. The duchess didn't have much of a say in it."

Sebastian shrugged, quickly tying his cravat from long practice. "She has a son, hasn't she? She's not completely alone at

Winstanton."

"That's another thing. Maggie says the old duke has made certain the son can't leave until he's of age. Rough for a mother to walk away in those circumstances."

Seb ran a hand over his jaw, satisfied the shave had been clean enough. He knew Dodds had a soft spot for Maggie and that he was repeating her side of the story. Who knew what the real tale was? When the memory of Catherine's words niggled at his conscience, he pushed them aside. It was none of Seb's business and he preferred to stay out of it. Didn't he have problems enough of his own? With a final glance at his reflection, he left his room to go downstairs.

By the time he entered the parlor, the other guests were already seated. They all looked toward him, which felt awkward. The mother and father of the child immediately began whispering together, while the child's wide eyes followed Seb to his seat. The older man and his younger companion were clearly not enjoying each other's company. Only Catherine smiled at him.

His gaze lingered on her lips, remembering kissing them only a short while ago, and the sounds of pleasure she had made. It might be more difficult than he had thought to keep his hands off her. Catherine's cheeks had pinkened as if she was remembering, too. She looked even more beautiful when she smiled, and it occurred to him that he had not seen her smile often. Despite her difficulties, Seb wasn't going to pity her, and he wasn't going to allow her plight to burrow its way into his conscience. He was no hero, and he certainly couldn't make everything better.

"What is happening?" he murmured, taking the seat beside her on the far end of the table. At least they had some privacy here.

Catherine widened her eyes dramatically, the smile still lurking in them. "There is a delay with our dinner. The farmer who was delivering the beef for the roast beef has had an accident. Benny thinks we are going to dine on bread and water, and when you opened the door, he thought you were Mr. Rose come to give us the bad news."

Just as she finished speaking, the innkeeper made a noisy entry to the room. "The roast beef will have to wait until tomorrow," he informed them in a jovial voice. "Tonight we have meat pie with potatoes. Just waiting for the crust to brown. And there's apple cobbler to follow."

There was a cheer from the child.

Catherine leaned toward Seb. "I don't know about you, but I am hungry."

Before Seb could answer, Miss Querol spoke up in a friendly voice. "I'm starved! I think it's all this waiting for the blood—I mean, for the weather to clear." Her blue eyes sparkled at her near blunder. "By the time we leave here I'll be as round as a ball. And in my line of work I can't afford to be fat!"

Catherine opened her mouth, looked at Seb, and closed it again. Mr. Querol was already scolding his "niece," who was unlike any niece Seb had ever seen. Wasn't the neckline of her gown a little too low, displaying her buxom curves? When she caught him looking, she winked, and Seb bit back a laugh. Whatever the relationship was between those two, it was far from filial.

He asked of the room in general, "Is there any word on how long the weather will keep us here?"

That brought forth a great many theories and speculations from the other guests. The boy, whose name was Benny, announced, in a voice much louder than Seb thought necessary, that he wanted to build a snowman. His parents smiled fondly at him and reminded him that it was too late to go outdoors.

"Tomorrow then," he said, pouting. He shot Seb a considering look. "Will you help me, sir?"

"Benny!" his mother said quickly, pink with mortification. "I do apologize, sir."

Seb laughed. "Of course I will help. Tomorrow though, young man. At the moment I am famished, and the duchess here is faint with hunger."

That was greeted with smiles and laughter, and when the food arrived shortly afterward everyone was quick to tuck in.

"There'll be supper later for those who want it," Mr. Rose announced when he returned with the pudding. "And don't worry, we can keep you fed for the next few days. But if the weather doesn't clear after that I might need to put you all on rations." He laughed heartily. "It'll be like being back in the army."

Sebastian looked up with interest. "Which regiment? I have friends who were fighting the French not so many years ago. One of them was at Waterloo with Wellington."

For the first time the innkeeper lost his smile, and the twinkle in his eye was replaced by something more serious. He began to regale them with stories of his time in the regiment and the places he'd seen, at the same time sensibly steering clear of anything that might offend the ladies or frighten Benny.

Finally, he said, "Do eat your pudding, sir. Before it's all gone."

Sebastian realized then that this may well be the case soon and hastily took a serving, pouring cream over the cobbler's cakey topping. Beside him, Catherine dabbed her lips with her napkin. Seb wanted to lean in and kiss her, taste her, and he quickly looked away.

"Are you really going to help Benny make a snowman?" she whispered. "If you're hoping he will forget then I'm afraid you'll be disappointed. In my experience, children never forget."

"I presume you're thinking of your son."

Her expression softened with affection. "Jack. Yes, he is a great one for insisting promises are kept. I promised him I would be home for his birthday." Her smile wobbled and her gaze dropped to the table.

"When is his birthday?" Seb asked gently.

"Only a few days. He will be six."

"Then let's hope the road is clear by then," Seb said bracingly. He couldn't help but ask, "What will happen if you can't fulfill your promise?"

Catherine grimaced. "There will be tears, I expect, and we will both feel terrible. And I will redouble my efforts to let him know he is the most important person in my life."

"Why didn't you take Jack with you to London?" Even as the words left his mouth, Seb regretted them. He remembered Dodds had said earlier there was some reason the son could not leave Winstanton, but at the time he had told himself it was none of his business.

Catherine fiddled with her napkin. "There were stipulations in my husband's will."

He waited but she said no more, and he suspected she was not keen to share the details. He might be her lover, but he was also a stranger. Or perhaps, like him, she just did not want to think uncomfortable thoughts. Time to change the subject.

"I swear to you I don't plan to sneak away and hide from Benny when the time comes to help with his snowman." He gave her his most charming smile. "Although you may need to give me some instruction. In *that* I am no expert."

Her eyes widened at the suggestive note in his voice. "I will be happy to help," she said firmly. "And I *am* an expert. In snowmen at least."

She was flirting. That sly upward glance from under her lashes, and the tilt of her lips. Seb might have groaned aloud if they were alone. His gaze swept over the freckles on her nose, and his pantaloons became uncomfortably tight. He wanted to encourage her to flirt more, but at the other table Benny was whining about having to wait until tomorrow for his snowman. His father took a firm approach. "It is far too cold now, and almost dark."

The boy wasn't happy about that, but he eventually saw the sense in it, especially when he was promised a storybook at bedtime. The family left the room, with a smile toward Catherine and Sebastian. The Querols rose too, but only so that Mr. Querol could move closer to the fireplace. He seated himself with a groan, stretching out his feet on the hearth. Miss Querol, or whatever her real name was, set her hands on her hips and gave him a glare before she shrugged and left him.

The room seemed peaceful now with just the two of them—apart from the sleeping Mr. Querol. Sebastian leaned in closer and the flowery scent of her soap made him want to close his eyes and just breathe her in. Tip up her face and kiss her until she was breathless and begging him to take her back to his bed. Kiss her delightful freckles one by one. As she turned her head he noticed a small mark on her throat where he had sucked on her skin a little too hard.

He'd marked her, and it gave him a guilty thrill. As if she was his when he knew she wasn't. Could never be. And for a man who was only passing time before the road opened, this way of thinking was very dangerous indeed.

Chapter Nine

AS HE MOVED closer, Catherine felt her heartbeat quicken and her skin prickle. Already her body associated him with pleasure, and yet they barely knew each other. He had been at his most charming a moment ago, to Benny and the others, and now that his focus was on her she was aware of just how intoxicating that charm could be. Her cheeks heated, and she shivered as his breath stirred her hair. There was a warmth between her thighs and an ache low in her belly, and she wanted him.

He made her feel like she never had before. She wanted more. For years she had longed for an interlude like this, with a man like Sebastian, and now that she knew exactly what she had been missing, she was torn. Before she had taken shelter at The White Rose, and fallen into Sebastian's arms, she had been resigned to living at Winstanton until Jack was twenty-one. She had been determined to swallow her unhappiness for his sake. But now . . . Catherine was struggling with that idea of a lonely, solitary life.

At the same time, was it a good idea to be making more memories when she knew their time together was finite? Wouldn't that just make her return to Winstanton more difficult? Even if it was a foolish decision, Catherine wasn't going to say no to him. She wanted as much of him as she could get. Her experiences at The White Rose could be stored up in preparation for the long, cold years stretching before her.

His breath brushed her ear again, and as though he had read her thoughts, he said in a deep growl of a voice, "I want you."

She closed her eyes. His fingers skimmed against hers where they rested on the table, and then he lifted her hand and pressed his lips to the curl of her knuckles.

"I can't get enough of you. I want to be between your thighs. I want my tongue inside you." His whisper filled her head with hot, delicious images.

She squeezed her legs together and his hand dropped to her thigh, smoothing over her skirts, cupping her knee. Her breath hitched.

"I could take you right here. Right now," he said, and the tip of his tongue followed the whorl of her ear. "And you'd let me, Duchess." He nuzzled against her throat.

"I . . . we can't." But her voice was feeble, and she was imagining him lifting her, spreading her thighs, and freeing his cock. The bulge beneath the flap in his pantaloons was obvious.

"You can," he said. He was drawing up her skirts, inch by inch, and in a moment he would have his hand on her bare skin. She ached, waiting, wanting his touch. He was seducing her with his words, and it was working.

Ah, there it was! His fingers stroked her bare thigh, moving upward while she shook and trembled. Those clever fingers slid between her legs and found the wet heat of her. She groaned, and pressed her face into his shoulder, biting her lip to stop herself from crying out as he rubbed her swollen flesh, dipping inside her. Again and again, building her desire to an urgent fever pitch. She moved against his hand, she couldn't help it, and he murmured approval and encouragement.

Then it happened. A wave of blissful pleasure, overtaking her mind and body, and stealing her breath for a moment. When she came to herself, he had removed his hand and rearranged her skirts and was smiling at her. The charming smile that warmed his pale eyes and curled his soft lips. Something inside her fluttered, not just desire but something more. Something dangerously close to infatuation.

Suddenly Mr. Querol gave a snorting snore, making them both jump. Sebastian's shoulders shook with laughter, and Catherine could hardly contain her own giggles. The weight of the moment had been lifted.

"Come to my room," she said decisively. She stood up and, when she reached the door, looked back over her shoulder. She made the gesture coquettish and for a novice she thought she did rather well. His expression grew more intent, and she had his full attention. Her breath grew a little shaky—that sense there wasn't enough air in the room—as she closed the door.

There was no one in the passageway or on the stairs, although she could hear Maggie's laughter from the kitchen at the rear of the building. With the early darkness closing in, the inn was full of shadows, and when she reached her room, Catherine lit a candle. The fire was still burning nicely, keeping her warm as she went to the window to draw the curtain.

For a moment she considered the bleak view from her windows at Winstanton—rocky ground and the moorland stretching away forever. The castle was old and drafty, and despite the fires that were kept burning in the main rooms, it stayed chilly. She had noticed how warm and comfortable her mother's house in London had been in comparison. If it weren't for Jack she wouldn't go home at all. But she couldn't abandon him.

He was an engaging child and yet his father had rarely spent time with him, preferring to ignore him whenever possible. In contrast, his Aunt Ellinor had loved him fiercely from the day he was born. Catherine could not fault the duke's sister when it came to Jack, although she was not an easy woman to know. When Catherine first arrived at Winstanton, Ellinor had kept to her rooms, barely speaking to her, running the house like an efficient ghost. After Jack arrived, things had changed. The two women had bonded over the child and now, although Catherine did not feel Ellinor was her bosom bow, she trusted her to care for Jack while she was away.

The knock on the door reminded her she was expecting a visitor. Memory of their intimate act of moments ago brought that ache back to her belly. How could she want him again this soon? But the truth was that she did.

As Catherine went to let him in, she realized she was smiling, and when she opened the door, she wasn't surprised to see that Sebastian was smiling, too. That teasing twist to his full, soft lips. Those oh-so-kissable lips.

Then he was inside her room, the door closed and locked behind him. His focus was on her as he drew her against him. Before she could speak, he bent his head and kissed her. It was not as gentle as his previous kisses, but it was certainly thorough, and it left her tingling and needy.

"I've been wanting to do that," he growled. Then, that intent look again. "Are you tender?"

"Tender? Oh!" It was new to have a man even think of such things. Catherine pushed aside embarrassment and considered the intimate question. She was a little delicate from where they had connected earlier, but it was definitely not enough to stop her from wanting him to do it again. She shook her head.

He looked unsure as to whether he should believe her. "Let us start with another kiss," he said, and this time his lips barely brushed against her own, over and over again. This was seduction, and she could feel herself falling under his spell.

He lifted his head, and when she tried to reconnect her mouth to his, he kept just out of reach, not allowing her to deepen the kiss. He continued to stroke her lips with his, clasping her upper arms, his thumbs making soothing circular motions against her skin.

It was gentle and considerate and . . . it was *torture*. Her breasts were swollen and aching for his touch as she leaned into him, and she whimpered with relief when his hand finally slid up between their bodies, and he cupped her rounded flesh. When he stroked the plump bud with his thumb she arched into his touch, wondering if it was possible to want him more this time than the last.

He kissed her again, licking along her bottom lip, and she opened her mouth and let him in. Oh, he was good at this. His kiss grew more passionate, making her head spin as he finished with the soft pressure of his teeth, once again on her bottom lip.

While she stood, dazed, he looked around and spotted the chair by the window.

"Undress for me," he demanded, an arrogant note in his voice.

And just like that the spell was broken.

"Undress for you?" The question was sharp. "So that you can see if I am perfect?" Her voice broke, as she felt herself suddenly swamped by the worst memories from her marriage.

Sebastian blinked in surprise and then his expression sobered. He could hardly miss her shocked expression, or the tension in her body as she tried to push him away. "Catherine—"

"Those times . . . he treated me as a cold and unfeeling thing. Less than a woman. Searching, always searching for a blemish, and if he found the slightest one . . . it was always my fault. He—he . . ."

Her voice wavered and she tried to hold the gush of words in. He didn't want to hear this, he didn't.

Sebastian reached for her, pulled her back into his arms and held her there. She was still tempted to fight him, but it was so nice here like this. The memories faded, and so did the threat of tears. Now that the duke was dead, she refused to cry over the past, but hearing Sebastian say that—she had felt so vulnerable.

"You felt powerless when he did that," he murmured against her temple. "But I won't force you to do anything. I am giving that power to you, Catherine. You can undress for me and make me want you even more than I already do. Or you can sit down and we can discuss politics." He huffed a laugh at the look of disappointment on her face. "*Or* you can seduce me, and I promise you I will be your willing victim."

She tilted her head back. Undress for him? *And for herself.* She imagined seducing him like that, watching him as he watched her, aware of how much he desired her. Teasing him, perhaps? A shiver of anticipation ran through her. She could do that, couldn't she? Take her husband's dominance over her and turn it about? It would be a remarkably apt way of exorcising those painful memories.

"Yes," she said. "I want to."

He searched her face, and when he read her resolve he smiled. "Good," he said, his voice deep and husky. He went to sit down in the chair, making himself comfortable, thighs spread, hands folded at his waist, and then he just . . . waited.

Catherine smoothed nervous hands over her skirts. She reminded herself that it wasn't as though he hadn't seen her naked before. She could still feel where his fingers had been inside her in the parlor. And this was her chance to practice something she may like to use again, when she found a man she wanted in her bed for more than a few days and nights. *Unless she had already found him.*

Swiftly she pushed that thought away and reached for the fastening of the high-necked collar of her gown. She had chosen it after she found a mark from his mouth on her throat, hoping to hide the evidence from the others. Briskly she began to undo the first button, and then the second.

His chuckle caused her to stop and stare. "You are meant to be seducing me," he drawled, "not trying to get this part over as quickly as possible." His heavy-lidded gaze slid over her. "Go slowly. Make me wait. Anticipation will increase the pleasure."

Oh. Of course. She took a steadying breath. When she reached up again, she took the pins from her hair, slowly and deliberately, allowing her dark locks to tumble down one by one. Then she set the pins down on the washstand and shook out her hair so that it was a dark cloud framing her face. He murmured something she didn't catch and shifted in his chair. She decided to ignore him and turned her attention to the buttons at her wrists, loosening the sleeves, before she bent over and slipped off her shoes, and put them aside. Just as he had done, she left her stockings. They would be last.

Back to her gown, and she reminded herself that this task was not to be rushed. This time she focussed on each button, and even took a moment to slide her hand into the open bodice, slowly, slowly, enjoying the sensation of her own fingers on her skin. This was something she never did. Undressing was just a means to an end, but now it was the act itself that was important.

She glanced over at him. Sebastian was focussed on her hands with an intensity that surprised her. He followed their movements, and then he shifted a little, opening his legs wider. The bulge between his thighs seemed to grow as she watched. He was aroused and it was her doing. Sebastian had been right, the power was all hers in this situation, and it felt good. Very good.

She finished with the buttons and allowed the top half of her gown to slide down, catching on her elbows. Her chemise still hid her breasts, but the points of her nipples showed through the silken cloth. She touched one of them, rubbing the peak, giving it a little pinch.

He groaned.

Encouraged, she did it again, finding the sensation so enjoyable that she could have continued for longer, except she wanted him to touch her, too. To feel his mouth on hers, on her body. Quickly she shimmied her gown over her hips and stepped out of it. Now there was only her chemise and her stockings, and she had his complete attention.

He murmured, "You're very good at this."

Such praise! From a rake no less. It sent butterflies flying in her stomach. Then she lowered her lashes coyly as she slid the straps of the chemise down over one arm and then the other. The tips of her breasts caught on the neckline for a brief moment before she was free, and the garment puddled on the floor at her feet.

He made a sound, a deep note of pleasure and desire. Of sheer want. For a heartbeat she thought he might leap up and ravish her, but that was not their agreement. When she looked again, he was cupping the bulge in his pantaloons as he watched her. The tight cloth stretched over the muscles of his thighs, and his shirt framed his broad shoulders and chest, and she wanted him. Badly.

She hesitated, not sure whether to continue or to go to him. What was the etiquette in these situations? She supposed she could ask him, but why not satisfy her own desires? She was in charge after all.

Catherine took a step toward him, gracefully, aware of her nakedness, the way her hair curled against the bare skin of her back and shoulders and the slight jiggle of her breasts. He seemed to be holding his breath. She was close now, and another step brought her between his spread legs.

He reached out and ran a finger lightly over her hip bone, and into the crease of her thigh. He continued around her body, finally squeezing the globe of her bottom with an appreciative sound. His gaze met hers. "It has been a long time since I felt this . . . this . . ." The words drifted off.

Emboldened now, she began to undo the fastenings of his trousers, leaning over him, and with a groan he took the tip of one breast in his mouth, suckling. Then the other. Her legs wobbled at the sensation and she reached for support. In a flash he had lifted her onto his lap, spreading her knees so that they rested either side of his thighs, and she was open to him.

She gasped as once more his finger slid into her damp heat, stroking, using the moisture of her desire to lubricate his busy fingers. She was more aroused than she could ever remember being, pushing back against those questing fingers as they delved again. He watched her face with a hooded, intent look. As if he already knew her body better than she. That attention was too much, too personal, so she closed her eyes and concentrated instead on his touch.

"Ah, you are ready again," he whispered against her lips. "Will you let me inside you, Catherine, so we can come together?"

Already that tension was rising within her, muscles straining, blood heating, heart pounding. She gasped out a "yes" and was aware of him freeing his cock. He rubbed the tip against her swollen flesh, and she opened her eyes to see him sucking on his fingers.

"You taste like nectar," he said, to her amazement.

He was easing inside her, and with a thrust of his hips went deep. His mouth covered hers, swallowing her moan, and she found herself eagerly pushing back. Taking as much of him as she could. Sebastian nuzzled at her throat and then took one of her nipples in his mouth, using his tongue, making that now familiar ache build and build.

She rose up on her knees, and when he withdrew this time, his cock rubbed against her sensitive bundle of nerves. It was enough to send her flying again, clinging to him and gasping. He thrust up into her, once, twice, and then he too went rigid, groaning against her shoulder for a long moment before his body went still and relaxed.

She could feel his heart beating against hers as they sprawled together in the chair, unable to move. Catherine wondered if she would ever be able to move again. The wonderful ache in her body. The sensation of his hand, rubbing circles against her bare back. His breath slowing, returning to normal, stirring wisps of her hair. And little kisses to her face, across her cheeks and her nose. So many little kisses, covering her in their sweetness.

Catherine didn't want to think. She wanted to let her thoughts drift into the darkness outside and fly among the stars, before falling to the snow-covered ground.

He brushed back her hair and sought her gaze. His own was more watchful than she had expected for a man whose body felt completely sated.

"Shall I ask for supper to be brought up here? We can dine

alfresco."

Was that a good idea? People would whisper about them, or be scandalized, well everyone apart from Maggie. But what did it matter, really? She would never see these people again, and even if she did, it would merely be a reminder of this moment.

"Yes," she said, smiling. "Let's do that."

Chapter Ten

DODDS AND MAGGIE brought the food, along with a small table and another chair. They moved about quietly, setting everything out, and then they removed themselves with a shared smirk and closed the door. Silence fell. It was, and Sebastian couldn't help but smile at the thought, *cozy*.

His smile wavered. He wasn't sure what he felt about that. He could not remember indulging in this sort of intimacy with any other lovers. Once they had extracted as much pleasure as possible out of each other's bodies, they had said goodbye. Sometimes the women lingered, but he soon disabused them of any idea of staying. Seb had never had a mistress tucked away, like so many other gentlemen did. The thought of letting someone down, of being responsible for their safety and happiness, and then failing . . . of losing everything all over again. It brought him out in a cold sweat. Better not to become attached.

But despite living his life exactly as he had wanted it for years now, he still wasn't happy. Lately he had felt a growing sense of dissatisfaction. Both the endless round of social engagements, and the women he bedded, had been reduced to a trickle. What had begun as a way to push aside his memories no longer did the job, and he wasn't sure what more he could do. Was there such a thing as happiness? Or was it unattainable for someone like him?

Seb's gaze rested on Catherine seated opposite him. She was wearing a silken wrap over her nakedness, but he could see the elegant line of her neck. Her dark hair had been twisted over one shoulder, to keep it out of the way as she ate. He watched as she reached for a cube of cheese from the platter before them, popping it into her mouth and sighing with pleasure.

Again, Sebastian wondered at this strange new version of himself. The intimacy of the moment was so comfortable, with none of the squirming in his stomach he usually felt. Nor the urgent need to get up and leave before he got too involved, to walk away and not look back.

Here he was, perfectly happy to lounge on his chair and sip the landlord's very nice red wine while he nibbled on thick slices of grainy bread, cheese, and cold meats. Neither of them had said much since the food arrived, and Dodds and Maggie left them alone. It didn't feel necessary to speak as their eyes met over the table and she smiled at him or he at her.

Perhaps his ease with Catherine was because he knew this to be a temporary arrangement? Or was it simply because he was sated, completely relaxed, without the energy to go anywhere? Better to believe that, he decided. Because if this woman had somehow slipped under his guard and pierced his heart, then he was in a great deal of trouble.

He picked up an apple and began to peel it. She seemed mesmerized by the adept action of his hands. Her eyes were as dark as the night outside, her lashes a perfect frame for their beauty, and something wrenched in his chest at the sight of her. He had never been much of a poet when it came to stringing together pretty words, but he wished now that he was, so that he could find some lyrical way to describe her.

Temporary, he reminded himself. That was the only word he needed to remember. They'd be parting ways soon and he would never see her again. And if they ever did meet, then he would pretend she was a stranger.

He supposed they *were* strangers. Although he now knew her body intimately, she kept a great many of her inner thoughts to herself. He did know she was brave—she must be to have lived through such an unhappy existence—and it hadn't made her bitter. When she smiled it was glorious, her face lighting up, her eyes shining, and he could imagine her in a setting different from the one she had been forced into. One where she was happy and content. Which was all very well, but he would never see that. Their paths would diverge and they would go their separate ways.

He handed her a piece of the apple he had prepared. Catherine smiled as she took it. "What is your home like?" she asked.

"You mean Albury House?" Strange that it was still *home* despite all his years in London and the tragedy that had sent him there. He stretched out his legs, stockinged feet toward the warmth of the fire. "My grandfather built it, and although it is solid enough to keep out the winter gales, it has some whimsical touches. There is a garden on the roof, and you sit up there and look out at the view. I used to do that, even when the weather was bad. Especially when it was bad," he added, with a smile. "There are a great many rooms—too many—but my grandfather hoped to have many grandchildren. Instead he had me. And now I am all that is left, or I will be when my father dies."

And he had said far too much now. He glanced up and found her watching him as she nibbled on her apple. She was doing that thing again, reading him, all but seeing through his skin. It made him uncomfortable but at the same time it was rather flattering that she was so interested. Most women took him at face value.

"You said you were going to see your father? Does he live at Albury House? If it is just the two of you, you must miss him when you are in London."

"Grimsley, my father's butler, sent me a message. A very brief message. He said that my father was ill and needed me, so here I am."

Did she know the details of his story? He was sure she did.

Winstanton would have delighted in telling her, or maybe she had heard it in London. People loved to share scandal and his was forever being recirculated through the *ton*.

She was still watching him and something in her gaze told him she *did* know, or at least knew enough. "It sounds like your father may have asked Grimsley to write," she said gently. "Perhaps he wants the past forgotten. Isn't that what you want, Sebastian?"

She was no longer pretending ignorance. At least she wouldn't ask him for his sad little story. He rubbed a hand over his face, pushing away the emotions that were building up inside his head. He rarely let them overwhelm him anymore—the regrets and the anger. But now, and he wasn't sure why, he could feel that situation fast approaching. Perhaps it was because he knew he would soon be at Albury House, or perhaps it was because the woman opposite him had also suffered. But even if she understood, he couldn't take the risk of letting her into his confidence, so he made his voice cool, polite, so that she would back off.

"I don't know if he wants the past to be forgotten. He has held on to it for this long. The reason I am going home is because I am his heir, and once he is dead there will be matters to be dealt with."

Her expression did not change, the kindness in her eyes, the empathy in her smile, but she must have read him correctly because he felt her take a step back. "Then I am sorry," she said. "Being forced to stay here, having your journey interrupted, must be very frustrating."

He stared, surprised, and then he grinned. "Not at all. This has been a most welcome interruption, Catherine."

She colored and her dark lashes swept down, almost shyly. He knew that wasn't the case, and he suspected she too hid her inner thoughts because it was painful to have them exposed.

There were two apples left on the platter, and she poked at their glossy skins with her fingertip. "It has been welcome for me, too," she admitted. "I have no choice but to return to Winstanton, and although I love my son fiercely, I miss . . . company. Sometimes I even miss my husband, ridiculous as that is, considering how unhappy he made me. But at least he was someone to dine with, to read to when he was at his worst, and to sit with in the long evenings. His sister Ellinor lives there, too, but she doesn't want to be my friend—she thinks my birth was too low for her brother—and when we do have conversations they are always about Jack."

"Do your mother and sisters not visit?" It disturbed him how alone she was.

"They have their own lives, and anyway I prefer to see them in London. It gives me an opportunity to get away. I was able to socialize a little this time." She looked up at him through her lashes, and her smile was wry. "My mother is trying to persuade me to marry again, but if I did I would lose Jack. She thinks it is as simple as taking him away from Winstanton, but it isn't."

"Do you want to marry again?" he asked in surprise. "I would think once would be enough to warn you off it."

That made her laugh. "How right you are." She turned one of the apples over. "Maggie thinks I should take a lover, and then I wouldn't be so alone. There was no clause in the duke's will about punishing me for taking a lover."

"Ah. But I imagine it would be difficult to be discreet. Everyone would know, and then if you broke off with your lover, everyone would know that, too."

Her fingers stilled and her eyes widened. "Exactly! If we fell out, it would be very awkward. Besides, I wonder now if I could be satisfied with a man who . . ." She stopped, bit her lip. "I don't want to risk Jack hearing the whispers. I would rather be alone."

Seb wondered what she had been going to say before she stopped herself. *A man who isn't you?* Was it insufferable of him to believe that? Catherine had opened herself up to him just now, shared some of her private thoughts, and it seemed only fair he share some of his own insecurities.

"I don't think I am made for the life of a country gentleman," he said. "Respectably married, a pillar of the community? There are reasons why that sort of cozy domestic life would not suit me."

Her voice had a mocking note to it. "Not enough variety? I cannot say I know a great deal about the lifestyle of a rake, but I imagine you would get bored very quickly if you were shackled to one woman."

That made him laugh. It was on the tip of his tongue to admit to her that for a year now most of his nights had been spent alone in his bedchamber. That the reason he was here with her was because he found her a refreshing change. Instead he said the sort of thing she was surely expecting him to say. "Tell me you are not naïve enough to believe marriage means spending your life with a single partner, Catherine?" He shook his head, and now he was mocking her. "Out of the bedchamber perhaps, in public view, but inside it? Certainly not."

She took a sip of her wine, seeming to ponder his words. "I know faithful couples among the *ton* are few and far between, but there are some. If I had my time again and I married a man I loved, then I think, I believe," she narrowed her eyes at his skeptical smile, "I *could* be happy with only him."

He didn't reply. He simply watched her, enjoying the way her hair fell in that heavy skein over her bare shoulder, and the swell of her breasts where the wrap had slipped lower. Her lips were reddened by the wine, and still a little swollen from their kisses. She was beautiful, yes, but there was more to it than that. She was endlessly alluring, and he had found her so from the moment she fell into his arms. He had expected, when he bedded her, that whatever fascination she held for him would vanish. It hadn't, and he wasn't sure what that meant.

One thing he was in no doubt of. He wasn't tired of her, or bored with her, or thinking of ways to escape. Quite the opposite in fact. He wanted her again. It came as a sudden, fierce longing that swelled his cock and made it ache. Perhaps his desire was so strong that she felt the tingle in the air between them, or maybe she was full of her own desire. When she glanced up at him, her wine-reddened lips lifted into a seductive smile, and their gazes held.

Outside the door, he heard the Fotheringham family pass by. They'd evidently been to check on their horse and equipage, and Benny's chatter in a high, excited voice, was interspersed by his parents' quieter tones. He wondered what his life would have been like if he had had siblings, or if his mother hadn't died like that. Would there have been a dynasty at Albury House? There was still time—he was only thirty-two. He could marry and father numerous children. And then what? Return to London and leave them behind? The thought made him want to squirm. What if he married Catherine and gave her another son to help her forget the one she could not take with her?

The idea shocked him, and not just because no mother would abandon a child and replace it with another. The shock was because he was thinking of Catherine as a prospective mate. It would never work for so many reasons. The notion that they might live together at Albury House in marital bliss was ridiculous and rather terrifying.

Now Querol and his dubious niece were passing by in the corridor. The woman's voice was perfectly clear, especially when they lingered just outside the door. "You paid for my company, my fine sir. You promised me a trip to Scotland. Now the weather's turned nasty you're finding fault with every word I say. I should return to London, where I'm appreciated."

"I don't want you to go back to London," Querol said testily. "I'd have you stay with me forever if you would only agree. I don't know why you want to carry on living like that when you could be comfortable with me, Anthea."

There was a silence, and then Anthea sighed. "We've been down this path. I know you think you want to keep me forever, but you'd soon grow tired of me. And then how would it be? We'd hate each other."

"Rubbish." But Querol sounded half-hearted, as though he'd had this argument with her before, and lost.

Her voice took on a cheerful note. "Let's just make the most of our time now. Do you think you're ready for another romp?"

Querol cleared his throat. "You know I'm not a young man anymore."

"You're as young as you feel," Anthea teased. "And I think I can get Little Master Querol up and ready. I know what he likes."

Querol made a sound suspiciously like a giggle. A moment later their voices faded and a door farther along the passage closed.

Catherine was choking with suppressed laughter, her hand covering her mouth. "Little Master Querol?" she said in a shaking voice.

Seb grinned. "Some men have pet names for their cocks. Didn't you know that?"

She laughed out loud this time. "What do you call yours?" she asked, dark eyes sparkling.

His grin widened. "That is between me and him," he said primly. Then he stood up, reached across the table, and held out his hand. With a lift of her brows she placed hers in it, and his fingers closed in a manner that was almost possessive.

The thought threw him, and the room seemed to rock queasily beneath his feet. She wasn't his, he reminded himself, and he wasn't hers. They were strangers, passing through The White Rose.

But the word "strangers" did not seem to fit them, not anymore. Their conversation just now had been satisfying if painful, the sort of conversation he might have with a valued friend. Someone he trusted.

Be careful. The warning sounded loud in his head, but for once he ignored it. His hand tightened on hers. He wasn't going to stop just yet. His body was greatly in need of hers, and at this moment that was all that mattered.

Chapter Eleven

EVERYTHING WAS STILL. Hushed. Catherine didn't want to open her eyes. She knew Sebastian was gone. She had slept through him rising, and dressing, and closing the door behind him. Why should he stay, after all? He'd had what he came for, but then so had she. They had given and taken pleasure such as she had only ever imagined, and in those moments she was closer to him physically than she had ever been to the late duke.

But despite that closeness to Sebastian, she barely knew him. She was sharing a bed with a man she barely knew, even while being with him was a revelation. He was not at all ashamed of his body and he never shied away from touching her and pleasing her—and himself. Spending time with him had made Catherine feel free in a way she had never felt free before. She was grateful for that; she'd never forget it.

But this was a temporary gift, and she was determined to look upon it as such, and yet . . . she would miss him.

She was not nearly as certain that he would miss her.

When she sat up there was a dent in the pillow beside her where he had lain that handsome head. Dreamily she tried to imagine the man as a boy. Women would have flocked to him from an early age, drawn by his looks and his charm. He must have grown used to such attentions, grown to expect them. He had said he could not imagine being married to one woman, that he had to be permitted to move on when he felt the need and not become mired in the minutia of domestic life. Which was sad because Catherine longed for those little things that made living with a man, a family, so special. The knowledge that someone loved you, and you them, that you could count on them to stay with you through the good and the bad.

Catherine needed that. Despite the unhappiness of her marriage, she had always needed it. She just wasn't sure such a life was possible for her.

It was certainly not possible with Sebastian, and she would be a fool if she allowed her hopes to be raised.

A shriek of laughter drifted up from outside. Slipping out of bed, she drew her wrap about her, noting the remains of their meal from last night had been cleared away. Maggie must have been in here, silent as a ghost, probably smiling to herself as she watched them sleep. She pressed her face against the glass pane to see below her window and found herself smiling too.

Benny, with cheeks as red as apples, was bundled up in coat, hat, and gloves, as he patted at the rounded sides of a very fat snowman. Or at least that was what Catherine thought the heaped pile of snow was meant to be. Mr. Fotheringham, his back to her, bent to scoop up more snow onto the already rotund form. But when he straightened, dusting off his gloves, Catherine realized this man was too tall and broad shouldered to be the boy's father.

Sebastian.

Yesterday he had promised to help Benny build his snowman, and she had teased him about it. She hadn't believed he had any real intention of following it through. Now she felt a little guilty for doubting him, because there he was, his deep laugh ringing out in accompaniment with the child's high-pitched squeals.

Seeing them together like this made something inside her chest squeeze so hard it hurt, and she put a hand to her heart as if it might be bruised. Was this the man he could have been if his life had been different? A father enjoying the company of his son?

Catherine couldn't seem to help speculating about him. She knew Sebastian was on his way home to Albury House because his father needed him. His father was ill. He hadn't said much more, only that he had been away for years and was only returning to see to the necessary arrangements when the head of a household died. He hadn't mentioned his mother, or what had happened to her, and Catherine hadn't asked, but she recalled the duke's words.

She was killed in an accident in a gig. Albury was driving.

"My lady?"

Catherine jumped. Deep in her thoughts, and with her gaze fixed on the domestic scene below, she hadn't heard Maggie come in.

Maggie smiled apologetically. "You slept late and missed breakfast *and* lunch. I can bring you some tea and toast. And I could arrange for Dodds to bring more hot water for a bath."

"No, it is late, and a wash will suffice. I am not hungry. I feel like all we do is eat."

Another shriek from Benny brought Maggie to join her at the window. She sniffed. "Is that a snowman? It isn't a very good one, is it? Master Jack could do better."

"Benny is having far too much fun to be worried about the look of the thing."

"The viscount could charm the birds down from the trees. All of the maids here at the inn are in love with him." There was something in Maggie's voice that made Catherine turn to look at her.

"I thought you said he was the perfect man for me. Don't you like him?"

Maggie looked uncomfortable. "It's not that. It's just . . ." She chewed on her lip.

Catherine felt her stomach sink. Had Sebastian been carousing with one of the servants? While he was with her, had he also been with someone else? But even as the thought came into her head, she dismissed it. For one there were practical hurdles, because when would he have had the time? But also because she suspected that, in his own way, Sebastian was too honourable to do such a shameful thing to her.

Maggie didn't notice her mistress' sudden silence, having come to a decision. "Dodds told me a story. About Albury's mother and what happened to her."

Catherine was almost relieved, and the words tumbled out of her. "Winstanton told me about that, too. He said Sebastian was driving the gig when she was killed. He was sent away from his home."

"Dodds wasn't there, and of course this was twelve years ago. But there's always gossip. It's said Albury was driving recklessly. They went right through the village at a clipping pace. Some folk said Lady Eltham was laughing and enjoying herself, while others said she was screaming and begging to be put down. Then as they turned to come back, the gig tipped over and his mother was trapped underneath. She was crushed and completely dead by the time they could get the gig off her. Albury was distraught, saying as it was all his fault. His father said it was his fault, too, and sent him off to London never to return. This is the first time he's been back since."

Catherine swallowed. It sounded like her father's death, but there had been no one to blame for that. It had been a terrible accident. Her gaze returned to Sebastian, and she tried to imagine him, shocked and repentant over his mother's death, only for his father to blame him and send him away. Had it been Sebastian's fault? Everyone seemed to think so. She did not believe Lady Eltham was screaming and wanting to be set down—Sebastian was not the sort of man to do something as ridiculous as drive an unwilling woman at top speed if she wanted him to stop. She remembered his care of her when he realized how the duke had treated her. But then his mother had died a long time ago, and it was possible he had changed over the years.

"I told Dodds he sounded like a wrong 'un, and I didn't want him near my lady, but he said he wasn't. Said it was his father who had got it wrong. Dodds knows Albury well, so I believe him."

Catherine managed a smile. "Thank you, Maggie. I did know the story, although not the details. I think this journey home is not an easy one for the viscount, but his father is ill and . . . maybe the earl wants a reconciliation."

"Or to give him another tongue lashing," Maggie said wryly. "I'll fetch you that water for you to wash in, my lady."

Catherine remained by the window as her maid bustled from the room. The story of his mother's death might explain quite a bit about Sebastian and the man he had become. No one could ever disregard their past, no matter how much they tried. It must have been terribly painful for him to lose his mother in such circumstances—she remembered losing her father—but then to lose his father and his home as well. She could not imagine herself without her mother and sisters, alone in the world.

His past explained why he might be reluctant to open his heart again. Not even to a woman who believed she could make him happy.

And it was none of her business. These were his private matters, and he would not thank her for involving herself in them, even if she might want to.

And Catherine found to her dismay that she did. Want to.

Chapter Twelve

"How are you feeling, Duchess?"

Seb was putting the finishing touches on the snow-man, but now he turned his attention to the doorway of the inn. Anthea had been watching them for some time, laughing and making comments, while Querol shook his head in his own grumpy fashion. Now Catherine had come to stand beside them.

"A duchess should be addressed as 'Your Grace'," Querol reminded Anthea in that fault-finding voice.

She ignored him, leaning in conspiratorially to Catherine. "You don't mind, do you, duck?"

"Duchess is a perfectly acceptable form of address," Catherine agreed. "Really, Mr. Querol, I do not mind."

Querol said nothing, but Anthea gave Catherine a look, up and down. Although Seb couldn't see the twinkle in the woman's eye, he was sure it was there. "We heard you was ill with a cold and were lying in, Duchess."

Catherine stumbled through her reply. "I . . . yes, I thought I did, but perhaps I just needed the lie in, because I'm better now." Her gaze flicked to Seb, and their eyes met for a brief moment.

He smiled. Anthea would be a fool not to realize what was going on between the two of them, and Seb did not think she was a fool. As if to prove it, she assumed a fake sober expression and said, "I always say there's nothing like sleep if you are feeling under the weather. And if you can find someone to share it with, then all the better."

Catherine flushed and now didn't seem to know where to look. Seb decided it was time to save her. "Duchess!" he called out. "Have you seen our dashing creation? Master Fotheringham wants him to have a name, but we are yet to agree."

The little boy was crouched at the base of the snowman, giving him a last pat, but he looked up now. "You *can* call me Benny," he said with a put-upon sigh. "We're friends now, aren't we, Sebastian?"

"I hope so," Seb replied agreeably. "We wouldn't want to fall out. We'd have to share this fellow between us then. Slice him down the middle."

Benny shot him a doubtful look and then ran a reflective gaze over the snowman. "I want his head," he said determinedly.

Catherine laughed. There was something light-hearted in their interaction with the child, and he liked it. Seb watched her walk around the snowman, inspecting him from all angles. They had found some horseshoes for eyes and a pinecone for a nose. There had been an old straw hat in the stables they'd purloined, and a tatty scarf from the same place to wrap around his neck.

"What about Benjamin for a name?" Seb suggested.

"That's *my* name!" Benny giggled. "And he doesn't look like me at all!"

"Hmm," Catherine tapped a fingertip against her chin in careful consideration. "What about Mr. Frosty? Flurry the Snowman? I know, Blizzard!"

Benny doubled over with laughter. Seb didn't think the names were particularly funny, but Catherine obviously understood children better than he. They were still tossing silly names back and forth, with Benny giggling, when Arnold Rose called out to them.

"Dinner is served!"

The Fotheringhams, who had appeared with the innkeeper,

hurried over to brush the snow off their son. Benny wriggled and complained at leaving his snowy friend, only to be reminded of how hungry he would be if he didn't eat. With a game of "guess what is for dinner" they persuaded him inside the inn, and the Querols followed. Leaving Seb alone with Catherine.

She was still smiling from the exchange with Benny. Seb pointed out that the base of the snowman was beginning to turn to sludge. "I think that's a good sign for the road north."

She didn't seem to hear him, and when she spoke it was to tease him. "You left me sleeping. I may still have been there if I hadn't heard you and Benny playing." Her dark eyes shone, and she looked particularly beautiful with her cheeks flushed from the cold.

There was that nuisance ache in his chest again. To give himself time to recover, Seb removed his many caped coat and shook it, melting snow falling from the folds. Beneath the coat he was in his shirtsleeves. When Benny had confronted him outside Catherine's room and reminded him of his promise, the child had been too impatient for him to do more than fetch his coat. Now he shivered as he slipped the coat back on, appreciative of its thick warmth.

"Maggie came to tidy the room and you were so deeply asleep it seemed a shame to wake you. The story about you having a cold was her suggestion. Everyone was most concerned, but here you are, hale and hearty and as good as new."

"Better than new, surely?" she said, her gaze on his.

He smiled a little helplessly. She had that effect on him. He opened his mouth to say the first words that came into his head— *I'm better than new, too*—but bit them back. They weren't appropriate, not when this was just a light-hearted, temporary thing. But the moment dragged on, and he couldn't seem to look away from her and the perfect picture she made against the grey sky and snow-covered ground. And yet she wasn't perfect, was she? She was human, the same as he was, with faults and imperfections. Like that sprinkling of freckles across her nose which made him want to kiss each and every one of them. Indeed he had done so yesterday, giving in to the impulse and scattering kisses upon her face like stars as she lay in his arms.

Perhaps she saw something in his eyes, or she didn't want him to see what was in hers, because she looked away, and went back to staring at the snowman. "You seemed to be enjoying yourself with Benny." Her voice was almost tender, and he supposed she was thinking of her son. "Children can be a joy."

"Benny's a rascal," he said, wrapping his coat tighter about him. His feet were numb and they needed to go inside, but he was reluctant to break this moment. "He has his parents wound around his little finger, despite their valiant efforts to keep him in line. And he seems to know just how far he can push them and always stops short of getting himself a scold."

"He feels safe. Not all children are lucky enough to have two parents who love them."

"Love doesn't last," he retorted, sounding harsh. His own childhood had been pleasant enough, and he had believed himself loved, until his mother was killed. How could his father have ordered him out of his home like that? Imagining Benny in his place, Sebastian didn't think he would be cruel enough to do such a thing. Deny his own child.

"Maybe it isn't meant to."

He looked at Catherine, forgetting for a moment what they had been talking about. Right. *Love.* Seb pulled himself together. "Maybe not. Seems a shame though, doesn't it? What is the point of all those famous lovers throughout history, pining and longing? If what they were feeling was just a waste of time?"

She shook her head at him, but she was smiling. "You are *not* a romantic, I gather?"

"I don't see the sense in it. Love brings grief, and grief is far worse."

She looked at him a little longer, and he waited to hear what she would say to that. Her smile was gone, and the sudden seriousness in her expression should have warned him that he was not going to enjoy whatever it was.

"I'm sorry about your mother," she said quietly. "I'm sorry that happened to you, Sebastian. But you shouldn't allow it to dictate the rest of your life. Painful things happen, but like the snowstorm that brought us here, they will eventually pass. Right now you are refusing to see the opportunities for love, for happiness, all around you. You need to open your eyes and your heart, or you will die a very lonely and miserable man, and that would be such a shame."

His heart was beating faster than he liked, and he wanted to swallow the lump in his throat. This wasn't good. She was encroaching on an area of his life that he never spoke about and tried not to think about. All very well for her to give him advice, but what did she know about his pain and suffering? And then he remembered that she did know. Catherine was a woman who had lived through a miserable marriage, to a man who was incapable of love. And yet here she was, telling him he could still live a life *with* love.

"Open my heart?" he scoffed, because otherwise he might do something idiotic, like fling his arms around her and sob on her shoulder. "I prefer to think with my cock, Catherine. It has served me well. Or are you complaining about that, too?"

She bit her lip. Had he shocked her? He'd done his best so that she would stop talking. "I am very glad for you then," she said at last in a wooden voice. "I hope you and your cock will be very happy together."

Ah, he had hurt her. Probably made her reassess her impression of him. Good. He didn't want her to think he was worth saving. And he certainly did not want her to think he and she could ever be a couple, because he suspected she was. Physical intimacy sometimes had that effect, but it was an illusion.

Catherine needed someone who would be devoted to her. A man to stand by her side and give her children, hold her hand when she was sad, and kiss her in their bed in the darkness. And love her. Yes, she needed a man who would love her.

And that could not be Seb. Could it?

An image flashed into his head, like a painting hanging on a wall in a happy home. Himself, smiling, standing beside her, their hands joined, Albury House in the background. It was pretty but it was a lie. It would never happen, and he wasn't about to fool himself into believing it could.

"Faster!" His mother's voice filled his head almost to bursting. "We need to go faster, Seb! Pretend we are escaping from a dragon and he is right behind us, his hot breath on our heels!"

She was always full of stories and games, the wilder the better, and Seb loved her for it. It balanced out the times she lay in her bed and told him dark clouds were circling her. When she was like she was today she made his life bright and alive, a counter to his father's more serious role. But Seb was also his father's son, and he had learned her erratic instants needed to be moderated. If he hadn't come with her today who knew what she might have decided to do?

"Not too fast, Mother," he warned. "This isn't called a 'suicide gig' for nothing."

She dismissed his warning. "We can't let the dragon get us," she said. "Here, let me take the reins. You are too slow, Seb. You must learn to fly."

The horrific sound of the gig overturning, the scream of the horses and then his mother's cries. And then nothing. At that moment the world stopped for Seb, and it never really started again.

Afterward Seb had blamed himself. He promised he would never inflict such hurt upon another, or allow it to destroy him, and therefore he would be alone. He would encase his heart in iron and no one would be allowed inside.

Yet here he was now, looking at Catherine, and thinking impossible thoughts. Of home and hearth and holding her in his arms all night. Of children who looked like him and her, and laughter and joy every day for the rest of his life. He wanted to double over and scream. He wanted . . .

"Sir?"

Dodds' voice shook him out of the madness. With its grip loosened, he was finally able to return to himself. The man he had become since he arrived in London. Cool and shallow and focussed only on pleasure.

He looked up, aware his appearance must be rather dreadful from the expression on Dodds' face, although to his credit he quickly hid it. "Yes, Dodds? What is it?"

"I asked if you were having dinner in the parlor or if you'd prefer another private feast?" Dodds' lips twitched as if the thought amused him.

Sebastian ignored it. "The parlor will do, Dodds."

He heard a rustle of skirts as Catherine walked past him and into the inn. She paused in the shadows beyond the doorway, and he wondered what she was thinking. Had she seen his raw anguish? The cracks in his mask? He did not show that part of himself to anyone, and the fear that she had seen made him feel unbearably vulnerable. To his relief she did not say anything, moving farther into the inn, until she was lost in the shadows.

He certainly wasn't going after her. In fact, it would do them both good if he absented himself for a while. Reminded her that they were strangers, soon to be parted. "On second thoughts," he said calmly to Dodds, "I'll check on our horses before I eat."

Dodds raised an eyebrow. "I've already checked on them, sir. They are being well looked after but I think they are raring to get going. Unlike me," he added in a mutter.

"We must not lose sight of the reason we are here," Seb said.

"Ah, yes. Sir."

Seb didn't take any notice of the doubtful reply and made his way toward the stables. Dodds called out again, asking about the meal, but Seb ignored him and kept walking.

He would spend a moment alone with the horses. It was what he needed. A chance to sort through his uncomfortable feelings and gather his thoughts. To repair the damage Catherine had done to his carefully constructed veneer. She may not have seen as much as he feared, but he thought she probably had. She was remarkably perceptive and that was all the more reason for him to distance himself from her. They had had their bed sport, but it was over, and once they left the inn he would not think of her. And he hoped she would not think of him.

Chapter Thirteen

S EBASTIAN HADN'T JOINED them in the parlor, where dinner consisted of the promised roast beef and gravy. The others groaned at the sight of it and tucked in with hearty appetites, but Catherine found she wasn't hungry, and even less so when it became obvious Albury wasn't going to come rushing in, apologizing for his lateness, and smiling at her.

It was her fault. She would never be a successful whist player. Her face showed too much, gave away her thoughts, and then her mouth joined in. And if that wasn't enough, she had spoken to him about *love*! As if he were Jack's age and needed guidance, instead of a grown man who lived the way he wanted to and knew his own mind.

Mrs. Fotheringham's voice broke through her thoughts, speaking to the room in general. "I heard Mr. Rose say we may be able to leave tomorrow if the weather stays fine." She turned to her son and added in a bracing tone, "Just think, Benny, we'll be on our way to see your grandparents!"

As expected, Benny whined, "I don't want to go."

His contrariness made Catherine smile. Jack was the same, although he was quieter in his rebellion. Sometimes too quiet. Winstanton was no place for a small boy, his only company two grown women and elderly servants. When she had seen Sebastian building the snowman with Benny, she couldn't help but imagine what it would be like if Jack were there, in Benny's place.

The door opened and she looked up hopefully, but it was only a servant bringing in more food. Some sort of custardy pudding with cream to go with it. Not Sebastian then, but she already knew in her heart he would not be joining them this time.

"At this rate I'll be getting as fat as Prinny!" Anthea exclaimed, eyeing the pudding greedily.

"Show some respect, woman," Querol growled. "To you he is His Royal Highness, the Prince of Wales."

"Pooh!" Anthea responded. "He likes to be called Prinny."

There was heavy silence as those present wondered whether she genuinely knew the prince personally, but no one was brave—or rude—enough to ask. Even Querol simply shook his head before he went back to his meal.

Catherine looked at the door again, her disappointment growing as Sebastian stayed stubbornly away. That moment outside, with the snowman and the long look that had passed between them—she had seen something in him that he didn't want her to see. Like a hidden door had been briefly unlocked and flung open, and she had a glimpse into his most private thoughts and feelings. It was only a moment and then he had locked the door up tight again.

Had she truly been thinking there might be a happy ever after with this man whose reputation preceded him? He was damaged, she could see that now. Whatever had happened with his mother and father had wounded him in a way that had not healed. Her words to him, although kindly meant, had peeled back the surface to expose his most painful memories, and she hadn't stopped there. She'd gone on, tearing into the exposed flesh. Pointless and cruel. He did not want to change. He did not want to play happy families, not with her or anyone else. This was a brief interlude, just one of many he had had before, and then he would move on. He had told her, he had *warned* her, and instead of listening she had allowed herself to begin to feel. To want to heal him.

Foolishly, she had allowed her longing for the impossible to ruin the pleasure she had dreamed about for years. He had even exceeded her hopes, and still she could not accept the finality of it. She kept wanting to turn it into something it wasn't and never could be. No wonder Sebastian had taken fright!

Giving up on her meal, Catherine pushed aside her plate, excused herself, and went upstairs. She had thought to spend some time alone, smoothing over her jagged emotions, but Maggie was there. She was busily tidying the room, while Dodds leaned against the windowsill and watched her. He straightened up abruptly when Catherine entered.

"Your Grace," he said, and made to leave, but Catherine held up a hand to stop him.

"Please, there is no need to go. I have come up for my cloak. I thought a walk outside might help blow away these megrims."

Maggie and Dodds exchanged a look that seemed to speak volumes. When had they become so attuned to each other?

Dodds spoke again. "I need to sew a button on one of the viscount's shirts, Your Grace. I wouldn't want him to look anything but his debonair best."

Catherine found a smile from somewhere, but he had already closed the door after him. Maggie helped Catherine into her fur lined cloak, but she noticed her maid was frowning as she tied the cords at her throat. "You will need your gloves, and your outdoor shoes. I think it is colder than it was before." She produced the required items and scurried about Catherine, helping her to put them on.

"I'm only going for a walk," Catherine protested, even though it felt rather nice to be fussed over. "I have a . . . a headache."

"You do seem out of sorts." Maggie rose to her feet once the shoes were in place.

"I think it is from being shut up indoors," Catherine said, ignoring her maid's skeptical glance. "Some fresh air will do the trick."

"Well, don't wander far. Would you like me to go with you?" Maggie's voice had taken on a worried note.

"I will be perfectly all right," Catherine insisted, putting an end to it by changing the subject. "Are you still enjoying Dodds' company? You seem very close. Almost as if you can read each other's minds."

Maggie snorted her usual laugh. "I'm not sure I want to read his mind. But we are enjoying being together. I think he imagines himself as the viscount's guardian angel, there to keep his master out of trouble. And there has been plenty of trouble, I can tell you." She chuckled to herself.

Catherine imagined some of the stories Dodds could tell about Sebastian's antics. The thought only depressed her more, and she made haste to leave her room and head downstairs.

Outside, the sinking sun was peeping through the clouds, which was a pleasant surprise, although the melting snowman looked rather sad. Benny would be disappointed, but Catherine lifted her face to the light with a smile, as she made her way toward the wood. To her surprise there was a path that was visible despite the snow on the ground. Perhaps the trees gave enough shelter to keep it from being covered completely. She walked deeper into the wood, aware of the deepening shadows but enjoying the stillness.

When she was young and lived in Hampshire, she used to walk to the farm near her home. To get there she'd had to make her way through woods and beside a stream, with the twittering birds her only companions. Her mother had been unwell for a time after her father died, and it had been up to Catherine to bring home enough food to get them by. Sometimes her sisters came with her, and their noisy laughter and bickering rang out as they walked. Ellis and Sophia had always fought, and Catherine had been the peacemaker.

The Mallorys might have been poor, near to destitute, but Catherine had accepted it. She had never expected more, and she supposed she had been happy. As long as they had food to eat and a bed to sleep in, she could bear the rest. Of course, she knew now that her mother had had much grander dreams, and once the letter from her cousin had arrived, offering them lodgings in London, she couldn't leave the past behind her fast enough.

"All we need is a foothold," Ellen Mallory had declared. "I can't accept that my three beautiful daughters are to be wasted on country bumpkins."

When they had arrived in London, it was Catherine who was dangled in front of the *ton*, with her flawless skin, soulful dark eyes, and her perfect profile. Her freckles were her only blemish, and her mother had despaired of them and tried all manner of remedies to make them vanish. And yet despite the freckles, Catherine had captured the wealthy old Duke of Winstanton and laid the foundation for her two sisters to follow.

She admitted to herself that the thing she yearned for most from her previous life was the simplicity of it. She had been happy, even after her father died, because she was with her family, and she felt useful to them. Then she had lost that closeness and been set adrift. Yes, she had Jack, but her title and the castle meant nothing to her. No doubt others would laugh at her unhappiness and call her ridiculous, but she had never wanted those trappings. And if occasionally she had thought being wealthy and a duchess might be nice, she had soon learned that without love it was meaningless.

By now the cold had seeped through her cloak, and she shivered, looking about at the monochrome landscape. The sun was sinking further and before long it would vanish beneath the horizon. Sometimes, at Winstanton, it felt dark for most of the year. There was a walled garden she had tried to grow flowers in but either the cold or hungry creatures had put an end to it. During her year of mourning, she had sat in the castle and it had felt like she was waiting, marking time, although she wasn't certain for what. Perhaps like in one of Ellis' silly books she was waiting for her prince to come and rescue her.

Well, he had not turned up because there was no prince, no

rescue, and it was foolish of her to imagine there was. Catherine knew very well there was only one person she could rely on to solve her problems, and that was herself. She had always known it, and she wasn't sure why she had begun to believe otherwise.

Jack was at Winstanton and she would return there, but things had to change. She could not live for the next fifteen years in that place as it was. She wasn't sure how to alter her circumstances for the better, but she would discover a way.

Feeling a little less fraught, Catherine turned to retrace her steps to the inn, only to give a start when she saw she was not alone. A little way from her stood a man with pale hair in a many-caped coat, leaning against the trunk of a tree and watching her. Just for a moment she imagined him an otherworldly creature, lurking in the encroaching shadows and ready to spirit her away. Her practical mind soon rejected such nonsense.

"What are you doing here?" she asked sharply.

Sebastian came to meet her, saying in his charming and amusing way, "Dodds told me you were out for a walk. He seemed to be under the impression you would get lost in the wood. Like some heroine in a fairytale, whisked away into the secret realm of the little folk. Or maybe you might encounter a wolf. I thought I'd best keep an eye on you."

She refused to be charmed, but she forced a polite smile. "This isn't an enchanted forest. And I was never in any danger of being whisked away or eaten by a wolf." *Was she?* Catherine glanced about her with a frown, and asked uncertainly, "*Are* there still wolves in the north?"

He chuckled. "No. It has been a long time since they roamed the countryside around here."

Silence fell. His presence made Catherine uncomfortable, and she wished he would go. Why was he watching her in that curious way? Her heart beat faster and suddenly that breathlessness was back. She didn't want to feel like this. She refused to feel like this. She needed to put some distance between them.

Catherine went to walk past him, but he reached out and

took her hand in his. She was so surprised that she let it lay there, unprotesting. He squeezed her fingers gently through their gloves, and this close she could feel his warmth through their clothing. Her treacherous body wanted to press against him, to have his arms about her and be held one last time.

She pulled her hand away, remembering that this was the man who had absented himself from the meal because she had dared to pry into his past. It had been wrong to do that, she admitted it, but his rejection still made her feel foolish and hurt, and she would not allow herself to be put in that position again. No matter how charming he might be when it suited him.

Sebastian's eyes were still on her face, and he had that pinch between his brows. As if something was worrying him, as if *she* was worrying him. "The groom says the road is clear to the south but not yet to the north. A tree fell across it and Rose has sent some men to cut it up and remove it."

"That is a relief!" she said, as he no doubt meant her to. "So we will be on our way tomorrow? Oh, I am so glad." Perhaps she was a little too enthusiastic.

"Our patience has been rewarded." The smile that curled at the corners of his mouth wasn't quite as charming as before.

She set a brisk pace back along the path through the wood. But if she thought he would let her go, she was wrong. He joined her, matching her steps, their boots crunching on the snow the only sound in the gloomy silence. In front of them the inn was a solid dark shape through the trees, with smoke curling from its chimney and swirling on the ground in a grey mist.

Catherine needed to say something. The silence between them felt loaded with words she must not speak. She did not want to cause him pain, or herself. What she finally blurted out was, "Maggie and Dodds have become good friends."

"Hmm." That frown again.

"Don't you approve?"

"No, it isn't that. I'm just surprised. Dodds is normally such a grumpy, solitary fellow. Your Maggie seems to have captivated him. I'm not sure what to make of it."

Catherine smiled. "Maggie has a way of captivating gentlemen. She then breaks their hearts without a second thought, but this time it seems different."

He grunted. Then said a little stiffly, "I apologize for not joining you for dinner. I was—"

"There's no need to apologize," she said quickly. "I have no expectations of you, Sebastian. You are entitled to do as you please. We are strangers after all."

She thought that was what he had wanted to hear but instead he gave her a swift look, his blue eyes questioning. If he was trying to read her thoughts he was out of luck. Over the years Catherine had become just as adept at hiding her feelings as he. Did he think she might break down and beg him to stay with her? Admit she had developed inappropriate *feelings* for him? Cause embarrassment to them both? Well, it wasn't going to happen.

Together they turned toward the front of the inn, and Catherine was certain this was the moment they would separate, so she was shocked when he turned to her and spoke in a diffident voice, no longer quite sure of himself.

"Will you join me in my room for supper? One final time, Catherine, before we leave."

She almost laughed, but he was in earnest. "Is this your cock talking?" she asked sarcastically. It was certainly not his heart.

He looked surprised. "Don't pretend we haven't enjoyed ourselves. Are you saying that if we had the time again you'd turn your back on me and sit alone in your room? Come, Catherine, admit it. Together we experienced a level of passion I will long remember."

It was true. She had enjoyed every moment of their time in bed. He had opened her eyes to the physical pleasures she had been missing all these years, and at the same time he had been patient with her. Understanding. It wasn't fair of her to blame him for not wanting a deeper connection. He had done as she asked of him, hadn't he?

Catherine had been going to refuse his offer but now she didn't want to. He was right, they had enjoyed each other, and she didn't want to sit sulking in her room. One last night with him, *that* was what she wanted. To make more memories she could store away for whatever future awaited her at Winstanton. What did it matter if she said yes? She would only be hurting herself.

She glanced up at him and away again. Her hands trembled as she tucked them beneath her cloak. "As you have asked so nicely, Sebastian, I will accept. One last night with the famous rake and then we are done."

He let out his breath, as if he had been holding it while he waited for her answer. "The 'famous rake' thanks you," he said, half laughing. There was a flush in his cheeks which must be from the cold, and his pale eyes glittered.

Whatever would have been said next was interrupted by shouts and horses' hooves pounding. An equipage raced along the road and drew up in front of them before the inn. Catherine stared. It was a curricle, something more familiar on London streets or bowling through Hyde Park than all the way up here. Mr. Rose came hurrying out of the inn, shouting to the stable boys and calling for servants to help with luggage. He was holding a lantern and by its light Catherine saw that the occupants of the curricle were a fashionable lady and gentleman.

"At last!" The lady threw off the blanket from her lap and jumped down to the ground. An oval of her face was the only thing visible within the fur lined hood, but she pushed it back and Catherine could see she was vivacious and pretty. She began to chatter nineteen to the dozen about the uncomfortable journey they had had from their last stop. The hostelry there had not been to her liking. "A *dreadful* room, you wouldn't believe the state of it."

"I can assure you that *our* rooms are clean and comfortable," Mr. Rose said smugly, waving to the stable boy to take the heads of the horses.

"I do hope so. The bed was distinctly lumpy." She looked restlessly about and spotted her audience. Her face lit up in recognition. "Albury? Is it you? What a pleasant surprise! If any man can take my mind off a lumpy bed then it is you!"

Catherine felt Sebastian's body tense beside her. An awful feeling came over her, and she just *knew*. She turned to him. He was staring back at the woman. "Do you know them? Do you know *her*?"

"Yes," he said, in a strangely cool voice, as though they had not just been discussing spending the night together. "I know her very well."

Chapter Fourteen

"THERE YOU ARE!" Seb said, as he entered his room. "Why are you never in the same place twice?"

Dodds stared at him. "I didn't know I had to be. What's the matter? Did you find the duchess?"

Seb had been in the stables when Dodds had sought him out to tell him that the duchess was wandering in the woods. Seb hadn't liked the sound of that, worry niggling at him until, despite all the reasons why he shouldn't, he had set off after her.

"Yes, I found her." He scrubbed his hands over his face as if to rid himself of something unpleasant. "I also ran into Lady Knowles. She and her husband have just arrived and are staying here."

"Knowles?" Dodds frowned. "Wasn't she one of your—"

"Briefly. It ended when I realized Lord Knowles was in the room next door, watching us through a peephole."

Dodds choked on a laugh, and then desperately tried to make his face sober when he caught Seb's sour look. "I remember now."

"I had invited the duchess here tonight, to share supper, but when she realized I knew Lady Knowles in a—a carnal way, she changed her mind."

"Oh." Dodds chewed on his lip. "How did she know about

you and Lady Knowles?"

Seb sighed. "Effie saw me and greeted me effusively. I don't think there could be much doubt in Catherine's mind."

"Isn't that a good thing?" Dodds asked. "This was always only a temporary arrangement with the duchess, that was what you said. This way she won't get any silly ideas."

Seb knew Dodds was only repeating what he himself had said. And Effie's appearance had certainly demolished his fears of Catherine wanting more than he was prepared to give. When she realized what his relationship was with Lady Knowles, her expression had shown contempt and her beautiful eyes had turned cold. "On second thought, I will eat supper with the others in the parlor," she had said, and walked off, leaving him standing there.

A pity it had happened just then, after he had persuaded her to spend one more night with him. Seb knew he shouldn't be disappointed. He should just shrug his shoulders, as he usually did when a woman flounced off, and put her from his mind. What was so different about this woman that he felt keenly the loss of that promised night? What made it feel so special and so precious that he could never replace it?

He blinked, aware that Dodds was rambling on about Maggie and he hadn't heard a word. "What was that?"

Dodds patiently repeated himself. "I said, the duchess' estate isn't far from Albury House, and I thought . . ." He examined Seb's expression and muttered, "I suppose I could go on my own."

"Why go at all? I thought you were a confirmed bachelor! And no, you can't go off on a social visit to see your paramour. Once we get to Albury House, we will stay for the bare minimum of time, and then return to London. You remember London, don't you, Dodds? It is your home and mine. This . . ." He waved his hand about. "This is the frozen, godforsaken north. Isn't that what you called it only a few days ago?"

Dodds' lips turned down and he looked like a sulky child. A

bit like Benny when he wanted something and was refused it.

Seb took a steadying breath. He put amusement into his voice to disguise the fact he was seriously concerned. "Are you really so taken with Maggie?" What if Dodds decided to follow Maggie rather than Seb? What if he abandoned Seb? He felt a little dizzy at the thought but reminded himself that, although Dodds' companionship meant a great deal to him, the man was not irreplaceable.

Dodds had paused, and for a moment Seb thought he was going to deny everything, but then he straightened, his shoulders back, and faced Seb like a man about to enter the boxing ring. "I am," he said. "She understands me. She allows me my silences and teases me out of my grumps. She doesn't mind when I'm not always smiling and chatty. She says it's restful."

Oh God, he really was smitten. Seb tried a patient tone. "Can you ask her to come to London with us? I could find her a position in my household." Although what she could do was a mystery to him, but it was a generous offer, and Dodds was aware of it. He seemed to relax a little, the tension going out of his shoulders.

"Thank you very much, sir. I will ask her, but . . ." That lowered lip again. "She is very loyal to the duchess. She will probably not want to leave her. You know she must remain at Winstanton? For her son's sake."

"Winstanton is a big bloody castle," Seb scoffed. "Hardly a hardship, Dodds. And I'm sure she has plenty of servants, as well as friends and neighbors, with whom to pass the time."

Even as he spoke he knew it wasn't true, and wasn't surprised to see Dodds shaking his head. "Maggie says the old duke didn't encourage visitors and didn't like her making friends. Frightened she'd find someone else, I reckon. He guarded her like a dog would a bone. And even though he's dead he's still keeping her prisoner, keeping the son hostage. Maggie wishes the duchess would just up and leave, but how can she?"

Seb imagined that depressing prison. He found that the

thought of Catherine alone and lonely was almost more than he could bear. He made his voice bracing, telling himself he needed to convince Dodds, but he suspected it was really himself he was trying to convince.

"Maggie is probably exaggerating. A duchess would have the means to ensure she was not lonely."

Dodds eyed him skeptically.

"Ask Maggie about the London idea and see what she says."

Dodds nodded and then, to Seb's relief, changed the subject. "Are you ready to go down to supper, sir?"

He rubbed a hand over his jaw; his facial hair was only a little darker than his hair, but he still liked to shave whenever he went out. "My last supper," he said with a forced laugh.

Dodds smiled dutifully.

Seb thought about that moment in the wood, when he had watched Catherine standing so still in her long cloak, gazing up at the lattice of branches above her as if she were casting a spell. Or perhaps she had already cast her spell, and it was on him. When she had turned around and noticed him, there had been no smile on her face and no warmth in her dark eyes. None of the sense of welcome he had felt previously. And he found he was sorry for that.

He'd hoped for one more night with her. In his arrogance he was certain he could melt the ice, explain what had happened with Effie Knowles and make her smile again.

"A change of clothing, sir?" Dodds' voice surprised him. Had his manservant been watching him all this time, reading his thoughts as they crossed his face? The idea made Seb feel uncomfortable.

He washed and changed, dressing in some of his town clothes. Tight pantaloons and a bright waistcoat over his white shirt. He combed his hair back with pomade, and Dodds gave him a close shave, so that his face was smooth to the touch. Afterward he felt more the thing. He might almost be off to some London club, and not out in the middle of nowhere with people he would never see again.

Now the road to the south was open, it was likely that the one to the north would follow by tomorrow. Seb could set off as early as he pleased and make good time to Albury House. He just needed to go. And no, he wasn't running away . . .

But he was. He was trying to outrun his confusing and uncomfortable feelings, which for some reason were no longer to be denied. And if he wasn't very careful he would actually have to take them out and examine them.

Chapter Fifteen

"MORE GUESTS!" MAGGIE said, when Catherine mentioned the new arrivals. "It's a wonder there are any rooms left."

"They are from London," Catherine said tonelessly.

"I saw them. Looked like they were determined to show the country yokels what real quality looks like."

Catherine forced herself to smile, knowing Maggie was watching her. She thought she might start to ask questions, but instead Maggie began busily sorting through clothing, folding the garments with more attention than usual.

"I haven't started to pack your trunk," she said at last. "I don't want to risk it in case it snows again." Maggie looked up and her face had lost its warmth. It was almost stark. "I'll miss him. It's silly, I know, I've only known him a few days, but he's grown on me. A bit like mold."

Catherine did laugh then. "So romantic, Maggie."

But she understood. Dodds and Maggie had a strong attraction to each other, and it would be difficult for them to separate. She wondered if Maggie would decide she'd rather be with Dodds than Catherine. What if she followed Dodds to Albury House? Catherine felt disorientated, as if the floor was moving. How could she manage at the castle without Maggie at her side? Her kindness and good humor, her generous spirit—it would be like losing one of her sisters. Worse!

Now, giving voice to those worst fears, Maggie said, "Dodds wants me to apply for a position with the viscount."

Catherine pushed back the rush of panic that was her first reaction. "Oh?"

"I said no, of course," Maggie went on matter-of-factly. "I wondered whether he could come to us instead. To Winstanton."

"*Oh.*"

"I know there is no gentleman he could valet, but he says he is a master of all trades. He could wait on tables or polish boots. I think he would make a first-rate butler, and the one you have is so very old. It must be time he retired."

It *was* time he retired. Catherine let the idea simmer for a moment. If Dodds came to Winstanton, then at least she would still have Maggie.

"What does Albury say? Has Dodds asked him?"

Maggie shrugged one shoulder, setting down a pair of stockings, but there was a stiffness to her posture that suggested she wasn't exactly easy with the thought. "I haven't mentioned it yet. I wanted to see what you thought of the idea first."

"I will help you in any way I can, you know that, Maggie. If this is what you want, and if Dodds is agreeable, then we can find some position in the household that suits him. Ellinor won't defy me; at least she had better not."

Maggie smiled at her fierceness, but her worried frown soon returned.

Catherine went to her maid and sat down beside her on the bed. Maggie kept her face turned away, seemingly wary of showing her feelings, but Catherine refused to be daunted. She knew Maggie, loved her as a friend, and even if Maggie wanted to leave she would not stand in her way.

"You have never shown any great interest in a man before," she said gently.

"I've never felt like this before. I didn't think I could." She shrugged again, as if her own feelings confused her. "Maybe it won't last. Perhaps I am as fickle as I thought I was, and someone else will catch my eye."

"Do you think that will happen?"

Maggie sighed. "No."

"You love him."

She half shook her head and then shrugged again. "I might. It seems far too soon to think of it like that, though. I need more time with him, and then I think I might love him. I am *falling* in love with him."

It sounded familiar, uncomfortably so, because that was how Catherine was feeling, too. She was teetering on the verge of falling in love, assuming she had not tipped over the edge already. And that was a huge mistake, because the man she was falling for could never love her back, and in the unlikely event he did they could never be together. Besides, she wasn't sure she wanted to be with him, not after that meeting with Lady Knowles outside the inn.

"You need to talk to Dodds," she said firmly. "Find out what he wants, and then tell him what you want, and perhaps between the two of you something can be sorted."

Maggie's eyes were brighter now, and it was only then that Catherine realized how dreary they had been. "Thank you, my lady," she whispered. Then, some of the brilliance fading, "But what about you? You are already so unhappy and—"

"Nonsense," she replied bracingly. "I would not let you stay with me if it meant you were miserable. I have known enough of that in my life, and I will not inflict it on others. Talk to Dodds and then we can discuss the situation."

Maggie nodded, but she was smiling. It felt good to have made her maid happy despite the sinking sensation in Catherine's stomach. She pushed it away and pretended it was hunger.

"I am ready for supper," she announced. "Should I change?"

Maggie considered the question seriously. "I think you should," she said. "Those London people need to see they are not as dazzling as they think they are. Wear the dress your sister had made for you."

Catherine stared at her. That dress was the most beautiful thing she had ever owned, but as she had pointed out to Sophia, she had nowhere to wear it. To which her sister had replied, "You don't need to be somewhere special to look special!"

"Isn't it a little too much for supper at The White Rose?" she asked eventually.

Maggie laughed in a wicked fashion. "Bugger that. Show the viscount what he is missing out on. I want to see the look on his face."

Catherine considered dressing up in that wonderful dress. Could she pull it off? Her pride had been badly dented, and if her heart was not already broken, then it was dented, too. Why not show him she was a desirable woman with a mind of her own? And, more childishly, punish him for disappointing her.

Chapter Sixteen

T HE DOOR TO the parlor opened and Seb sat up straighter in his chair. He was gawping and he couldn't stop himself. Catherine was wearing a gown the color of blush pink rose petals, the candlelight rippling across the satiny cloth as she moved. It looked almost made of water, flowing about her. Her dark hair was dressed simply, but she did not need artifice with her beauty. She looked so stunning he couldn't think of a word to say, and it wasn't often that Seb was struck dumb.

It was a moment before he realized the others in the parlor were equally lost for words. He was about to rise to his feet—it seemed like the thing to do—but Lord Knowles was there before him. Knowles had already greeted him with the mocking comment that he looked like he was on his way to a ball in Mayfair. Seb had ignored him beyond the usual courtesies, and since then Lord and Lady Knowles had been talking in loud voices, dropping the names of persons they were acquainted with in London, as though it was paramount that they impress the other guests and make them feel inferior.

Seb had heard Anthea snigger a few times when Querol gave a muttered aside. The Fotheringhams looked completely out of their depth, and Benny had been silent. Their happy little troop was no more.

"Who is this glorious creature?" Lord Knowles asked, though it sounded more like a declaration.

Before anyone could answer, Benny shouted out, "That's the duchess and you should call her Your Grace!"

Knowles frowned, but thankfully Rose arrived before he could give Benny a set down. The innkeeper had overheard the conversation. "This is the Dowager Duchess of Winstanton, who is staying here with us," he said proudly. "Your Grace, have you made the acquaintance of Lord and Lady Knowles? They've just arrived."

Lord Knowles gave him an impatient look. He had obviously been about to flatter Catherine even more ridiculously before the interruption put him off his stride.

"How do you do?" Catherine said faintly.

Effie Knowles smirked. "I saw you when we arrived. With Albury."

"The road to the south is open," Rose interrupted again, beaming at them. "And those of you journeying north should be able to leave in the morning. We're expecting the mail coach. Once we hear them blow the horn, we'll know for certain the way is clear."

"I am acquainted with your sister, Your Grace." Effie Knowles ignored the innkeeper and beamed a smile of her own.

Catherine replied, "Sophia knows everyone."

Seb bit back a grin as Effie was silenced. She was a vibrant woman, always dressed in the height of fashion and with plenty to say. She was also an unrepentant flirt. She had offered Seb a great deal but her delivery in the bedroom had been disappointing. Especially when it turned out it was a show put on to titillate her husband.

Seb's gaze went to his lordship. He was smiling at Catherine too, but his smile was far from that of a gentleman making her acquaintance for the first time. There was a word for that look, and it was lascivious. Seb watched as Knowles' gaze slid over Catherine's bosom, nicely framed by the bodice of her dress.

Some men thought women existed only for their pleasure, with no other purpose, and Edward Knowles was one of them.

For a worried moment Seb wondered if *he* was like that. It was true he was an admirer of women, but he would never expect them to dance to his tune just because he might want them to. His enjoyment depended on their pleasure being mutual.

It was time for him to join the conversation.

"Surely The White Rose is too far from the capitol for the two of you? What are you doing so far from London?"

Effie smirked and simpered. "We were in Derbyshire when we were invited to a house party. It didn't seem much farther north but the weather and the dreadful roads have conspired against us. If we had known, we would have declined—this is not at all what we are used to! But there were some very tempting inducements." Her smile grew. "We couldn't say no, could we, Edward?"

Edward took his gaze off Catherine's bosom long enough to grunt.

Effie had already tried to get Seb to sit down beside her, but instead he had taken the smaller table, saying untruthfully, "I beg pardon, but I usually sit here." Effie had looked put out. He only hoped that Catherine would pick up on his cue and sit beside him or he would be left in solitary splendor.

Now she hesitated, her gaze searching for an alternative, but the only other vacant seat was the one beside Effie. It seemed that Seb was the better option, and she took her place beside him.

Once again Effie appeared disgruntled. "Well! I see now why you refused to sit beside me. Never let it be said I stood between you and the duchess, Albury."

The way those bright eyes slid from Catherine to himself, full of speculation, was particularly unpleasant. He noticed Catherine's hands were shaking as she unfolded her napkin. Why had the wretched Knowleses to come now and spoil what had been a very nice tryst? Yes, things had gone a bit awry at the end, but Seb was sure he could have smoothed it over. He was very good at talking his way out of a difficult situation. Now everything felt painfully awkward.

The food arriving was a pleasant distraction, and everyone had to make the important decision between soup with bread and butter and soup without. When that was done, the only sound to be heard was whispering between Lord and Lady Knowles, a cackle of laughter from Anthea, and Benny whining that he did not like the soup and what were those "bits" in it?

As Catherine took a sip, her gaze slid sideways and she caught Seb watching her. She set down her spoon and raised her eyebrows inquiringly. "Do you have indigestion?"

That made him laugh under his breath. "If I were prone to it, then this would be the moment. But no, there is nothing wrong with my digestion."

She looked as though she didn't believe him, and he decided he should try some honesty. He had nothing to lose, after all. "Lord and Lady Knowles are the sort of people I avoid when I am in London."

"And yet she seems to know you so well." She picked up her spoon again, and then put it down. "Were you lovers?"

This was more frankness than he had expected! Seb wasn't used to being questioned over his choice of partners, but in this instance he wanted to answer. It felt like the right thing to do, and at least Catherine wouldn't think as badly of him as he feared she did now. Why it mattered *what* she thought was a topic he didn't want to explore.

He bent his head and lowered his voice even further so that Catherine had to lean into him, their foreheads almost touching. It must have looked intimate from the other table, but he wasn't going to share his secrets with everyone.

"Last year I made the mistake of spending a couple of nights in Lady Knowles'—Effie's—bed. Her husband knew about it. When I cornered her on the subject, she admitted that he encouraged her liaisons. Not that there is anything wrong in that if both parties are agreeable, but in this case I had no idea I was bedding Effie for Edward's pleasure."

He waited for her response. Would she be surprised or shocked or amused? But her face was politely blank, her eyes still fixed on his. Seb noticed again how long and thick her lashes were, and the way her freckles made a faint splash upon her skin. He was feeling uncharacteristically nervous as he continued.

"She also admitted that Edward was watching us from an adjacent room. A peephole had been specifically built into the wall so that he could observe. It made me feel . . . grimy. I am no saint but there is something unpleasant in the way Edward encourages his wife to sleep with other men so that he can watch. It isn't a game I want to participate in."

Catherine frowned. He thought she would ask him more about Effie and Edward, but instead she turned the conversation to him. "Then you do have rules when it comes to your partners? Principles? I imagined a rake would be willing to try anything. Is there such a thing as a Rake's Code of Conduct?"

Behind him he could Effie chattering away, dropping names like confetti, trying to convince everyone that she was quality with a capital Q. "So you know Prinny, too?" he heard Anthea ask drolly, and the gasp that followed.

He concentrated on Catherine's question. "Despite what you may think of me, I do have rules *and* principles. These days . . . even before Effie, I was finding the life of a rake, that sort of life, had run its course. It has been a while now since I involved myself in such debauchery."

Until you. But he left that unsaid because his time with Catherine did not feel like debauchery. It did not feel like anything he had ever felt before.

She stared at him in that manner of hers, like she was trying to read his mind, but he did not look away. Let her look, let her see he was not the sort of man she had obviously thought him to be. Then her expression softened, and he wondered if she would change her mind about tonight after all. Anticipation, the memory of her body against his, the way she had muffled her cries against his shoulder in this very room when his hand was between her thighs, made him shift a little in his seat.

Then Benny piped up behind them. "Will there be time to make another snowman before we leave?" His parents' murmured response obviously wasn't what he wanted to hear, because he called out to Seb. "Sebastian! Can you make another snowman with me before we leave?"

Unwillingly, Seb took his attention from Catherine and turned around. "I think the snow is melting, Benny. We will have to wait until next winter."

As the boy bemoaned his response, Seb's gaze went unwillingly to the Knowleses. Effie was smirking at him, but Edward was still staring at Catherine. That look on his face! He was imagining tupping her. Fury boiled up in Seb's chest and it was all he could do not to stand up and demand the man step outside. One thing he was determined on: Knowles was never going to get his hands on Catherine. Even if Seb had to sleep outside her door all night, that lascivious blackguard was getting nowhere near her.

"Will you be staying here again next year?" Benny hadn't finished with him yet.

"Benny, please stop it. The viscount has other plans and so do we." His mother tried to divert him.

"What other plans? Are we going to London, like Anthea said?" He fumbled a little over the name, which caused Effie to snigger.

Anthea came to his defence, shooting daggers at the other woman. "You should, Master Fotheringham. There is so much to see your eyes will be as big as dinner plates."

The child's eyes were big enough now, as he questioned her about the various attractions. Seb couldn't help but smile at his enthusiasm and added a few suggestions of his own, much to Benny's delight.

Who cared that Effie was watching with a sneer on her face,

or that her husband must consider him a lost cause? A renowned rake chatting with a child? But Seb enjoyed being with Benny, and he had enjoyed allowing himself to be silly and childlike. It was almost like he was rediscovering the boy he used to be, before hurt and suffering turned him into a man whose only pursuit was pleasure, his only need to forget.

In that moment he wondered what sort of man he would have been if his mother hadn't died in that awful way. How would his life have turned out? But he didn't go down that road. Such reflections were foolish and a waste of time. He was what he was, and there was no way of going back. All he could do was go forward and see where that led him.

Chapter Seventeen

CATHERINE'S THOUGHTS WERE in a muddle. She was glad that Sebastian had told her the truth, even if hearing about the Knowleses' sexual exploits rather shocked her. She was an innocent, she supposed, despite Sebastian's tutoring. Would he suggest she lie with another man and let him watch? She did not think so. He seemed quite possessive, with those irate looks he kept sending Lord Knowles' way. His lordship was the sort of man she would never have anything to do with, but it was amusing that Sebastian was being so protective.

And rather flattering.

Then there had been Sebastian's conversation with Benny, him winning the child over as he did everyone. He was kind, and it did seem he had principles. Just when Catherine had decided she was done with him and must hold him at arm's length, she found herself falling under his spell again.

With supper over, the guests began to leave to return to their rooms, but before she could follow them, Sebastian placed a hand on her arm. When she looked up at him in surprise he said quietly, "Will you change your mind about tonight?"

It would be easy to say "yes," and she could pretend it meant as little to her as it did to him, but it would hurt to do so. And then she would have to hide the hurt. She was tired of pretending to be a woman she wasn't. "Surely you have shown me every-thing?" she said, to give herself time find an answer.

He gave her a wicked grin. "Barely scratched the surface," he said in a gravelly voice.

Ah, now that *was* tempting. She was weakening again, think-ing that perhaps one more night would be worth any heartbreak she might suffer afterward. As she hesitated, Catherine noticed that a third person had joined them. Effie Knowles, her pretty face creased in smiles as her bright, malicious gaze went from one to the other.

Sebastian noticed her too, and Catherine couldn't help but be further amused at his irritated expression.

"Fancy! Albury making snowmen with the children of com-mon folk," Effie declared airily. "Who would have thought?"

"Perhaps you do not know me as well as you think you do."

Her eyebrows arched. "I think I know you very well. Every part of you, Albury." Then, resting a hand on his upper arm, she leaned in close so that she could whisper in his ear. "Will you come to me later? You won't be sorry."

The words weren't so quiet that Catherine couldn't hear, and she suspected she was meant to. Was he going to agree? She hoped not. Only a moment ago he had said he would not, but that didn't mean he couldn't change his mind. Effie probably knew what he liked without him having to worry about her inexperience. Catherine was painfully reminded of the yawning gap between them.

She made a move toward the door. "I should be packing. I intend to leave early in the morning."

But Sebastian blocked her way, his tone almost desperate. "Wait."

Effie gave an affected giggle. "If you're worried the duchess will be bored without your company, rest easy, Albury. Edward will entertain her." She inspected his face and said nastily, "Oh! Are you jealous, Sebastian? Have you lost your heart to the duchess? The ladies of London will be *devastated*. Wait until I tell them."

Sebastian's expression darkened. "My heart is as safe as it always was. Nothing has changed. Tell the ladies of London that, Effie."

Catherine wanted to escape and yet she felt compelled to stay, to listen to this awful conversation, even while her own heart began to crumble. Sebastian had shown he despised Effie, but this was a reminder of what he was, how he had lived his life despite insisting his life of debauchery bored him. Words easily spoken when he wanted to persuade Catherine into his bed but easily forgotten as soon as he returned to London.

"As for Edward, tell him to keep his breeches buttoned." He was towering over Effie, but she just giggled again, and flapped a beringed hand at him.

"Oh pooh! You enjoyed our little threesome. I dare say we could make it a party of four. What say you, Duchess?"

This time Catherine turned away without answering, but again Sebastian followed her, closing the door on Effie, and leaning against it. The handle turned, and they heard her complaints from inside, growing more and more shrill. Sebastian ignored them.

"I know I have spoiled whatever was between us," he said urgently, "but I want to make it better."

She wished she could trust him, but Effie had reminded her that she couldn't. "Your private life has nothing to do with me," she said coolly. "Why should I care? Why should you?"

"I've explained what happened with Effie and Edward—"

"Do you think I might invite him to my room instead of you? Isn't it all the same?" She was goading him, and it gave her a twisted pleasure when he blanched.

"No! At least . . . this is different."

She looked at him with surprise. "How is it different, Sebastian?"

He opened his mouth, closed it again, as if he didn't know what to say. But that was the problem, wasn't it? He was not equipped for a situation like this. He didn't want to hurt her, she understood that. He wasn't a cruel man. But how could he not hurt her when they were so different, each of them wanting different things?

Catherine found her voice. "This was a mistake. I shouldn't have started this. But I wanted to know what it was like to enjoy the company of a man I desired, and you gave me that. Thank you. You are a high mark against which I will measure all others. But I need more than carnal pleasures. I want someone who will love *me*, and not look for the next prospect when he is bored. You have helped me to understand that, Sebastian, to understand myself, so thank you again."

He stared at her, the pupils in his pale eyes enlarged and making them oddly dark. "Catherine," he said, and then couldn't seem to think of anything more.

"Sebastian," she interrupted gently. "I hope all goes well with your father. I know you want it to. I think if you can make your peace with him, then everything in your life will be better."

She turned and left him there, with a furious Effie pounding on the door. As she walked away she could no longer stop her tears blinding her and spilling down her cheeks, but at least he couldn't see them.

Chapter Eighteen

ONCE HE HAD opened the door for Effie, ignoring her stuttering rage, he went upstairs. Dodds was busily packing, ready for their escape in the morning. He looked just as miserable as he had earlier, during their conversation about Maggie, but this time Seb thought it best to ignore it.

"Why are the Knowleses here?" Dodds asked. "I forgot to ask before. A bit far from their usual hunting ground, isn't it?"

"They're going to a house party."

Dodds gave him a hard stare. "Tell me you're not going, too?"

Sebastian glared at him. "Of course I'm bloody not!"

Dodds tipped his head to the side, seeming to read something in his face. "His lordship has his eye on the duchess, doesn't he? Of course he does. She's a beauty. He'll want his wife to keep you busy while he—"

"I won't let that happen," Seb said stonily. Then, when Dodds was silent, "He doesn't know her."

"Neither did you until a few days ago."

He wasn't sure what to say. As with Catherine moments ago, the right words wouldn't come. But Dodds was right, he hadn't known her except as a memory, so why did it feel as if he did? As if he had known her always?

Dodds went on curiously. "The Knowleses are here, and your past has risen up to bite you. A pity. The duchess seemed to like you despite everything. And she sees you, the real you, even when you try to hide your feelings. The you I remember from the night I wouldn't let you into that club and we stood talking. You were drunk, I grant you, but you talked about your life and your feelings. You were alive then, sir. Far more alive than you are these days."

"Rubbish," Seb muttered the word. "How would you know?"

Dodds shook his head. "I know you better than you think. You're bored and you're looking for something, but you don't know what it is or how to find it. And then, when it presents itself right in front of you, you want to run away."

Dodds had gone far beyond the scope of his job, and Seb could dismiss him right now. Of course he wouldn't, no matter how angry his manservant made him, because they were more friends than servant and master.

"It's good to know you are such an expert in character assessment," he said nastily. "May I suggest you look to your own faults rather than mine?"

"At least I know when I see a good thing. I'm not going to let Maggie get away from me. I'll fight for her. What are you going to do?"

There was a lump in Seb's throat as he remembered the look on Catherine's face outside the parlor door. Why the bloody hell had he said that to Effie about his heart? Catherine must have thought he was a lying coward.

"What can I do?" he asked, not sure whether he wanted an answer, but Dodds gave him one anyway.

"That's up to you, sir. You can go back to London when you've finished at Albury House and put the duchess out of your mind. Or you can try to persuade her to give you another chance."

True, he could run away again, but he had grown weary of his life in London and the distractions that never lasted. But with

Catherine . . . he already knew he would never grow tired of her. She was a source of endless fascination to him. But more than that, he wanted to make her smile. He wanted to make her happy. But how? He would be sure to fail and hurt her, and then they would both be miserable.

Thankfully, Dodds left him alone after the lecture. Seb lay in his bed, knowing he would have a long day tomorrow, but he couldn't sleep. He got up and searched in his case until he found the message Grimsley had sent him. He had reread it so many times, and yet he did so again, wondering if there was something he had missed. But the meaning hadn't changed. His father was ill and Seb was needed. Well, tomorrow when he arrived home, he could discover for himself what state his father was in and whether a reconciliation was possible.

As he lay back, deep in thought, he heard footsteps farther down the passage, followed by a knock. Not on his door. Was it Catherine's door? He sat bolt upright, the message from Grimsley fluttering onto the floor. Seb leapt out of bed and pulled on his robe.

Outside, the passageway was dim, only a candle with a glass chimney to shed light. Quickly he made his way down to Catherine's room and knocked. There was silence inside, but he could see the glow beneath the door. Was she ignoring him? He was tempted to shout and hammer on the door, but that was so out of character that it alarmed him, so he didn't.

Thinking that perhaps she didn't realize it was him knocking, he said, "Catherine? I only want to talk. Please open the door. I want to apologize . . ." But there were so many things to be sorry for he couldn't even begin to list them.

But she didn't open the door and there was no sound from behind it, and after he had lingered another minute or so in awkward silence, he turned away. Only to discover Effie Knowles standing behind him in a thin wrap and, if the candlelight behind her was to be believed, nothing else.

She swayed toward him. "No luck then, Albury? What a pity.

I believe my husband got there first. But I am still more than willing to help you pass the time until they are finished."

He put up his hands to stop her getting any closer and said in a rough voice, "I'm not interested."

She pretended not to care, but he could see the flash of hurt and anger in her eyes. "Your loss." She didn't try to stop him as he stepped around her and headed back to his room, where he closed the door and leaned against it.

His thoughts were racing.

Was Knowles really with Catherine? She had told Seb she wasn't interested in the man, and yet . . .

Was this a jealous rage tearing at his insides like claws? The very thought of Catherine and Knowles made him want to break something and scream out his fury. And that was frightening, too, because he was never like this. He was known for being amiable and easy-going, with a live and let live philosophy. Even his worst detractors tended to like him. This just wasn't him.

His room felt like it was closing in on him. Where was Dodds when he needed the man? With Maggie, probably, plotting to run off together. He took a deep breath and then another, knowing he was being ridiculous but unable to help it.

"What is happening?" he muttered to himself. "Why is this happening?"

Dodds' words echoed in his head, even as he tried to remind himself that he had never wanted the sort of life Catherine spoke of. *Love?* It was a messy emotion he had avoided ever since his mother died. Since he'd killed her. Since his father sent him away, blaming him without listening to his explanations, and not caring what happened to him after that. He had been determined to live an independent and solitary life, enjoying the physical indulgences available to him but never allowing anyone to hammer through the iron encasing his heart.

And yet Catherine had managed it. She had torn away those heavy metal plates and now he was in unfamiliar emotional territory. Confused and out of his depth, floundering in waters that may well drown him.

There were two options before him. Run away or face up to the truth. The thought of returning to his comfortable life in London, each day the same, the years passing, was suddenly so unbearable he felt nauseated. But facing the truth about his feelings for Catherine . . . asking her to trust him with her happiness, with her heart, when he wasn't at all sure he was worthy or capable of that trust?

Sebastian groaned and threw himself down on his bed.

Assuming she wasn't cozying up with Knowles in her room right now, allowing that man to kiss her and touch her. The strange rage he had been feeling a moment ago threatened to overwhelm him again, but he pushed it aside. She wouldn't do that. She wasn't the sort of woman who would take a man she disliked so heartily into her bed.

I want someone who will love me, who will not look for the next prospect when he is bored.

Sebastian groaned again. That someone could have been him. Was it too late? How was he going to convince Catherine when tomorrow she would be gone? With no intention of ever seeing him again.

Chapter Nineteen

CATHERINE'S HEAD ACHED. She had barely slept, tossing and turning, and before that listening first to Lord Knowles and then to Sebastian knocking at her door and asking to come in. Perhaps it would be funny one day, but right now it was far from that.

When she told Sebastian she had learned a valuable lesson from her time with him, she had genuinely meant it. She *needed* love. Pleasure was all very well, but love was at the top of her list. What she hadn't told him was that she was falling in love with him, and it hurt unbearably to know he could not reciprocate.

Watching Effie Knowles trying to lure him back into her bed made Catherine furious. How dare the woman? Yes, Sebastian had refused her and appeared genuine in his declaration that he would not allow her into his life again. And Catherine believed him despite his reputation. So, if she believed him, what was the matter with her? *Jealousy.* It was embarrassing to admit, but Catherine was jealous because she wanted Sebastian for herself.

He had been her dream man for years, so that when the real one arrived, handsome and charming, it was easy to fall in love with him. He was easy to love. He made her feel like the most important woman in the world, and she forgot about the long list of others. With his focus on her alone, his past did not matter.

She was like a wilting flower, finally given some water.

And they could be happy together! She knew it. If he hadn't locked away his heart—and despite what he'd said to Effie, she knew he did have one. She had seen for herself his struggles to keep it contained. Yes, his heart was sensitive and bruised, of course it was. He had been deeply wounded by his father's abandonment of him and his mother's death, and he had decided never to love again. He stubbornly held by that decision no matter how miserable it made him. Catherine couldn't mend him—he had already rejected her interference once. He had to make that decision himself. Perhaps it was too late for him to change. Perhaps he preferred the life he knew to the one he might have.

It didn't matter. Even if he found happiness one day, it would not be with her. Their race was run, and soon she would be leaving The White Rose and they would never see each other again.

Eventually time ticked on, and the first glimmers of dawn shone through her window. There was the sound of a coach approaching. It rumbled along the road from the south, and as it passed the inn the driver blew on his horn so loudly she covered her ears. The mail coach, hurrying past. Going north.

She knew what that meant. The road was clear, and it was time for her to go.

Catherine threw back the covers and went to the window. There wasn't much to see. It was barely light, and the trees across the road from the inn were silhouetted against the sky, ice daggers on their branches. As she watched, a robin redbreast flew down onto one of them, and sat a moment, as though contemplating the day ahead. The sight lifted her spirits, and she reminded herself that no matter how bleak things seemed there was always something to look forward to.

She would be home soon, and Jack would be waiting. She would be there in time for his birthday, and they could celebrate together. Ellinor would probably be glad to see her too, and they could discuss estate matters. Ellinor had always been the chatelaine of the castle but perhaps it was time to change that? Catherine may not be able to find the happiness she longed for, but she could make her mark, rule her little kingdom in the north, until Jack was old enough to take over.

If she couldn't be happy, then at least she could be busy.

When Maggie arrived with hot water flustered and looking like she had dressed in a hurry, Catherine did not remark upon it. She washed and donned her traveling clothes, ready to make one final appearance at breakfast. She intended to press some coins into the palms of the serving maids and thank Mr. Rose for making her stay so comfortable.

And she wanted to say goodbye to the Fotheringhams and Anthea and Mr. Querol. She rather thought his grumpy demeanour disguised a kind nature and a deep love for his companion. Then there was Sebastian.

She would not waste her disappointment on him. He was what he was, and she had accepted it as she lay mulling over their time at the inn. They had shared some truly wonderful and pleasurable moments, or at least she had thought they were shared. Maybe for Sebastian they had been nothing out of the ordinary. And then she told herself it did not matter—she would never forget even if he did. He would live on in her dreams.

Maggie looked tired as she arranged a shawl to best effect about her mistress' shoulders. Catherine made her voice gentle when she asked, "What has Mr. Dodds decided?"

Maggie gave a laugh that was far from her usual joyful sound. "Mr. Dodds isn't very happy with his master right now. He says that Albury is a stubborn fool, and I don't think it would take much for him to decide to run off to Winstanton with us. But Albury House is not far from us, so he says he will visit me as soon as he can."

"Well, at least you have that to look forward to," Catherine said bracingly. When Maggie gave her a worried look, she pretended to be searching for a handkerchief and avoided her eyes.

Breakfast was already underway, with everyone there apart from Sebastian and Lord and Lady Knowles. Anthea was quick to share the information that the two Knowleses were still asleep in their room. "In no hurry to leave, those two." She pulled a face at Catherine and then lowered her voice a little, although it didn't stop everyone around them from leaning in, agog to hear. "That gent tried to press me against the wall last night. Horrible breath. Not that I'd want him anyway when I have my little bear." She squeezed Mr. Querol's arm and watched fondly as he blushed. "I think you've guessed he is not my uncle. He's asked me to stay with him always, and I have a mind to do just that."

Catherine was happy for her and for Mr. Querol, who was nothing like a little bear, but love did strange things. Benny was in the dumps, but talk of his snowman cheered him up. "You have been ever so kind," Mrs. Fotheringham said. "Our stay here has been such a delightful one." Because the Fotheringhams had arrived the earliest for their breakfast, they rose the soonest, hurrying up to their room to collect their belongings. It was sad to see them go. Catherine now thought of them as friends.

She had finished her coffee and was just about to rise and say her goodbyes, when the door was flung open and Maggie stood there, wide eyed. Behind her was Dodds, looking equally concerned. It was such a surprise that just for a moment all she could do was stare back at them, wondering what on earth was wrong. Was it Sebastian? Had something dreadful happened to him?

"What is it?" she cried, clumsily pushing back the chair and getting to her feet.

"My lady." Maggie stopped, bit her lip, and started again. "I'm that sorry. The wheel on your coach is broken. Dodds tried to fix it with the help of the groom, but the axle is bent. He says we need a blacksmith." She glanced helplessly back at Dodds and he put a reassuring hand on her shoulder and gave it a squeeze.

"There's a smithy in the village," he said, "but no one knows how long it will take for him to do the work. Seems he's busy. So many coaches and gigs and the like have come to grief in the bad weather. And your coach is very old, Your Grace. Could be it is not able to be repaired."

Maggie looked somber. "Looks like we won't be going anywhere today after all, my lady."

Catherine opened her mouth and closed it again. Her first suspicion was that the two of them had planned this, but it was short lived. She knew Maggie, and the dismay on her face was genuine. And what of Jack? She would miss his birthday tomorrow and he would be so upset. Tears sparkled in her eyes, but she blinked them back.

"Well," she said, taking a breath and trying to sound optimistic, "we'll just have to make the best of it I suppose. I'll ask Mr. Rose if he can accommodate us for a little longer."

"I'll go and ask him," Maggie said, but before she and Dodds could leave, Sebastian arrived. He was in his traveling clothes and looked weary, too, with shadows under his eyes. His gaze went from Dodds to Maggie, and when they repeated their news, he stilled. His eyes seemed to brighten, and his mouth twitched at the corners.

It was almost as though . . . as though he was *glad*. Catherine had barely registered this fact before he rearranged his expression into something approaching sympathetic. "That is most unfortunate," he said, in a serious voice. "And as Dodds says, who knows how long it will take to fix your coach with so many other broken equipages waiting for attention? You could be here for, well, *weeks*. And I know how eager you are to get home."

"The coach is ancient," Maggie said with a grimace. "I was surprised it got us this far."

"My late husband saw no reason to keep it in good repair or purchase a new one when we never went anywhere," Catherine admitted. She was watching Sebastian suspiciously.

"It rattles something awful," Maggie added.

Dodds was staring at his master. "I have a feeling you have

solution to this catastrophe, sir," he said in a droll sort of voice.

Impatiently, Catherine looked from one to the other. "What solution? Are you a blacksmith now, Albury?"

"Not quite. But I do have a perfectly working coach, with not a rattle in it. Why don't you and your maid come with us to Albury House? As you know it is a day's ride from Winstanton, and I'm sure my father has a suitable vehicle for you to use to continue with your journey. If not, then you can take my coach."

Catherine stared at him. Her immediate thought was: *No. Definitely not. I am not going anywhere with you.*

He must have read her answer in her face because he redoubled his effort to persuade her. "I refuse to abandon you here at The White Rose." And then he added slyly, "Not with Lord and Lady Knowles as company."

She flinched. He was right, the last thing she wanted was to be left here alone with those two. Could she bear another night of Lord Knowles knocking on her door? Remembering she was not alone, she looked up and saw that Mr. Querol and Anthea were watching with interest, and Anthea had a twinkle in her eye.

"Master Jack's birthday!" cried Maggie, only just remembering. "You can't miss it. He'll be inconsolable. If you go with the viscount you can reach Winstanton by tomorrow, and still be in time."

If there was the faintest hope of her reaching the castle in time for Jack's birthday, Catherine knew she must take it. All the same she felt beaten, forced into a situation she did not want, but she had to make the best of it. She lightened her voice when she wanted to growl. "Thank you, Albury. I accept."

Sebastian's shoulders relaxed, and so did Maggie's. "Thank God for that," she muttered.

"But we will leave for Winstanton as soon as we arrive at Albury House," Catherine went on quickly, expecting an argument. And at the same time she resolved to pretend to be asleep the whole way, to avoid any uncomfortable conversations with Sebastian. Or to remember how painful it was to be with him when she could never have him.

Dodds gave a sideways glance to Maggie. There was a grin hiding behind his battered face, and Catherine had the feeling he wanted to jump for joy. Maggie nudged him with her elbow and he huffed out a laugh.

Sebastian spoke again. "We will get to Albury House tonight, but it will be late. The northern road is clear according to Rose, but the turn-off through the village to my home may not be in such good repair."

"You mean we may get stuck for the night?" Catherine gasped. She was thinking of being trapped with Sebastian in a perilous situation and maybe her thoughts were visible on her face. Sebastian's mouth twitched again as if he wanted to smile, but he brought it under control.

"Never fear, if it becomes necessary, we can unharness one of the horses and Dodds can ride ahead and bring help back for us."

"I certainly can," Dodds agreed much more cheerfully than Catherine thought necessary.

"And then we can go straight from Albury House to Winstanton?" Catherine wanted an answer.

"Of course," Sebastian assured her brightly. Then his face fell in a way she was sure was more theatrical than genuine. "However," he gave a grimace, "if it is very late you may have to stay until daylight. It would not be safe to go on in the dark." He shrugged, as though the outcome was out of his hands, and of course it was. Catherine knew then she would be staying at Albury House tonight whether she wanted to or not.

She glanced at Sebastian again, as he began giving instructions to Dodds about bringing down the luggage. Why did she feel Sebastian was pleased about this change in circumstances? Surely it was as much of an annoyance to him as to her? If he was hoping to use the journey to talk to her, persuade her to spend tonight in his bed, then it was not going to happen. But why would he want to? Hadn't they already discussed their situation and reached a mutual understanding? There was nothing left to talk about.

"I am only agreeing to this because of Jack," she said firmly. "He is the only reason."

Sebastian stopped what he was saying to Dodds and gave her a bow, and what was meant to be an understanding smile. "Of course, Duchess," he said.

There was a gleam in his pale eyes, and Catherine didn't trust it or him. He was up to something, and she would have to be on her guard.

Chapter Twenty

SEBASTIAN WAS WIDE awake as they approached Albury House. Catherine was asleep, with Maggie dozing beside her. Dodds had ridden most of the way outside with the coachman, saying they needed two pairs of eyes for such a journey. It had been as expected, slow and cautious. Although they had passed abandoned carts and other vehicles on the side of the road, they hadn't ended up in a ditch, so that was something. Once they had turned off what could loosely be termed the northern "highway", things had been a little more nerve-wracking. Night had fallen, but Sebastian had known they were not far from home.

And this was his home, despite the length of time he had been away and the circumstances of his leaving. As a child, as a boy, in good times and in bad, he had loved this place. To his surprise he rather thought he still did.

It was dark, but the storm clouds had long since cleared away and the moon shone down. They passed by the wood where Seb had helped his father replace the fallen trees and listened to the earl's hopes of a future when Sebastian's own children would climb them. There was the fence his mother had jumped over on her mare, and he could almost hear his father's voice as he told her to be careful. Sebastian had laughed, thinking it a great joke. Once, when he was a child, they had picnicked on the lawn, and his parents had fallen asleep in each other's arms. Seb had watched them, half asleep himself, and thought how lucky he was.

And then at last they turned onto the circular drive at the front of the house, and he saw that everything was in darkness. He was so used to London hours, he had forgotten this was the country, where folk went to bed early. But the darkness was not quite complete because there was a single light burning in an upstairs window, and it was a relief to know someone was awake.

Seb climbed down from the coach, and stretched his stiff body, before he went to ring the bell that hung beside the door. The sound was loud in the silence. When no one came, he rang it again, and the agitation inside him grew.

Catherine and Maggie were descending from the coach with Dodds' help, and their voices drifted toward him. He was here, he was home, he had answered Grimsley's summons. Why was no one waiting to let him in? Had his father forbidden him entrance to his own home?

When the door was finally answered, it was by a servant he had never seen before, a nightcap on his head and a robe hastily thrown over his nightshirt.

"Do you know what time it is?" the man demanded grumpily.

Sebastian wasn't going to put up with that. "I am Viscount Albury here to see my father. And you are?"

The servant's eyes widened in shock. "Sir . . . I apologize, sir. You weren't expected. No one knew you were coming."

"I don't know why. I had a message from Mr. Grimsley to come at once. Unfortunately, the storm held me up and . . ." He stopped. "Never mind that. Where is Grimsley? And where is my father?"

The man's eyes grew even wider, probably at the thought of waking them and explaining why he hadn't immediately welcomed the son and heir into the house. "They're in bed, sir! Everyone's abed. We keep early hours here." Then, seeing the expression in Sebastian's eyes, "In—in case you've forgotten."

Seb wanted to ask more questions. Wasn't his father at death's door? That was the impression he'd had from Grimsley. Had he been misled? He needed to get to the bottom of this, and he needed to hear it from the butler's own lips.

"Get Grimsley down here," he ordered. Then, remembering his guests, "No, on second thought, get me the housekeeper."

The man looked like he wished he could sink into the floor. "She's not here, sir. She was called away by her sister before the weather turned, sir, and hasn't returned."

Why was nothing going to plan? And why was he standing out here? He pushed by the man and strode into the house, leaving the servant to scuttle after him. Instead of the house giving him a sense of warm homecoming, it felt even colder than outside. He wanted to shout orders for all the fires to be lit at once, but one thing at a time.

"The Duchess of Winstanton and her maid are to stay here for the night. Their coach broke down and they will continue their journey to Winstanton tomorrow. I want the best rooms prepared for them."

The man bit his lip, clearly out of his depth. "The *best* rooms? I'm not sure . . ."

Seb might have exploded then. He was fast losing whatever easy-going charm he had left. But a touch on his arm made him turn to see that Catherine had joined him without him being aware of it. Her dark hair was loose around her shoulders, she seemed to have lost her pins, and her face looked pale and exhausted. And then he realized that with all his staring he'd missed what she'd said and had to ask her to repeat it.

"*I said*, instead of yelling at this poor man, perhaps you could find a female member of staff who can help?" That last she addressed to the servant, who gave her a belated bow.

"Of course!" he said, relieved to be told to do something he was able to do.

"Leave the lantern," Seb growled, when the man moved to take it with him. "And fetch Grimsley too! For God's sake," he muttered as the servant's steps faded into the gloom. The place was in chaos. Even with country hours there should have been some preparation made for his arrival. Why had no one expected him to come?

Impatiently he took off his coat, and then wondered if he should have left it on. It was bitterly cold in here, with the bone-deep chill that spoke of no fires having been lit for some time. He couldn't let Catherine freeze after he had persuaded her to come here with him. Seb looked about him, and then nodded toward a door to his left. "We'll wait in there." Adding under his breath, "Who knows how long the fellow will be?"

The yellow sitting room had always been his mother's favorite room, and he hoped it was in a fit state after all these years. To his relief, as he held up the lantern to inspect it, the room appeared much the same. The fire was out and from the look of it, hadn't been lit for a while, but there was a neat pile of wood in a basket on the hearth. Dodds knelt and saw to getting the fire going. Maggie was yawning but quickly covered her mouth when she caught Seb's eye.

Catherine was drawn closer as the flames caught, and she held out her hands with a shiver. "Can we go on to Winstanton tonight?" she asked, worried dark eyes finding his.

"No, best to wait until tomorrow, Your Grace." It was Dodds who answered. "Luck brought us this far, but we wouldn't want to push it."

Seb expected her to argue but she let it go. Instead, she turned to him. "I thought you were expected. Why was there no one to greet you?"

Sebastian met her dark eyes and saw the genuine concern. She cared about him. The knowledge made his chest ache in that curious way he was starting to grow accustomed to. "I didn't reply to the message Grimsley sent me. I just . . . set off. Perhaps he thought I wasn't coming. And now I'm wondering if my father is dying after all. Surely if he were, there would be a doctor and a nurse, and . . ." He stopped, an appalling thought occurring to him. "Do you think I'm too late?"

Catherine drew closer. Her cloak brushed against him, and she stared up at him, reading his face. "Oh, Sebastian," she said. "I do hope not."

He shook his head tiredly. "I don't think he's . . ." He swallowed. "The servant would have said, surely?" For some reason he was looking to her for reassurance, and Catherine did not let him down.

"Yes, he would have said." She put her hand on his arm and squeezed. "Why don't you put your coat back on? It's very cold in here."

"I must speak to Grimsley. Where is he?" He glanced about as if the butler had appeared while his back was turned.

"Don't worry about us," Catherine said briskly. "We will sort out somewhere to sleep. It's only one night after all, and you have more important matters to be—"

Her words ended in a soft gasp as he reached for her, drawing her into his arms. He didn't care that they weren't alone. He just needed to hold her close. She was warm and soft, and just the feel of her bolstered his spirits and calmed his fears.

"I'm a terrible host," he murmured into her hair. "I never imagined things would be like this. I hope your castle will give you a better welcome than my home."

She didn't pull away, and in fact her body seemed to melt into his. "No, you're not terrible at all. And how were you to know? I'm sure things would be worse if I'd stayed at The White Rose with that awful . . ." Her voice trailed off.

He leaned back so that he could see her face. "That awful . . .?" His mouth quirked. "Do you mean Effie Knowles?"

"She *is* awful." It was Dodds who spoke up, making the two of them jump.

"Proper cow," Maggie added. Her eyes were twinkling as Catherine eased herself away from Sebastian.

Dodds took note of his master's expression. "We'll go and see if the rooms are ready," he said hastily and, taking Maggie's hand, led her from the room. As the door closed there was a burst of laughter.

Catherine avoided Seb's eyes, and when he reached for her again she side-stepped him. "I must get home," she reminded him a little breathlessly. "I promised Jack. He'll never forgive me if I—"

"I am not arguing with you," he said, although he sorely wanted to. "You can set off early tomorrow morning. I will even send Dodds with you."

Relief made her smile. "Thank you. Although I'm sure it will be a terrible hardship for him to come with me and Maggie."

"As long as he doesn't stay," Seb grumbled, and her smile broadened.

"This is a nice room," she said, glancing about at a spindly-legged table and chairs and the desk by the window. The walls were decorated with paper, a cream background with tiny yellow flowers, and portraits and landscapes hung from the picture rail.

"My mother's room," Seb said abruptly. "It looks exactly the same as it did when she was alive." Almost reluctantly he went to the desk where she used to sit. His heart gave a thump. There was a half-finished letter laying there, the pen waiting in the inkwell for it to be completed.

It was then he understood that his father had left everything exactly as it was on the day his wife had died. The realization made him feel shaky. He had known his parents were deeply in love, and he knew his father had been devastated when she died, but he hadn't comprehended quite how long his father had been in mourning. He had been thinking of his own misery, wallowing in his own feelings, and rightly so. But perhaps he should have spared a thought for the earl.

Catherine was watching him, that warm understanding in her eyes. "Does the window have a view?"

"It looks over the rose garden, or at least it did. I'm not sure whether the roses are still there."

"A rose garden would be perfect." She spoke dreamily. "Yellow roses to match the room."

He tried to pull himself out of his funk. The least he could do was meet her halfway. "Yes, there were yellow roses and purple lilacs. I remember—"

The knock on the door was loud enough to startle them both. Seb called out for whoever it was to come in.

The door opened on Grimsley.

Seb's first thought was that the man hadn't changed. He had been old when Seb left and he was still old. Those woolly eyebrows had always had a life of their own. But as Grimsley shuffled toward him, Seb could see that he *had* changed. He was more stooped and his grey hair hung down to his shoulders. Yes, he may have been called from his bed, but he was not the spick-and-span butler Seb remembered.

Just as Seb began to wonder if he should introduce himself— had it been so long?—the butler's face broke into a warm smile, and he reached to take Seb's hand in both of his. "They told me it was you, Master Sebastian, but I didn't believe them." His voice was croaky. "I didn't think you'd come. I hoped you would, but after . . . well, who could blame you for holding a grudge? And you may not have felt you were welcome." His eyebrows dipped down at the memory of that fateful day.

"And yet here I am." Seb returned the warm handclasp. "And now I want to know why you told me my father was ill."

Grimsley returned his gaze in silence, considering his reply, and Seb saw that his brain was still as sharp as ever. Then the old man sighed, as if he was too weary for speech, and shuffled toward the fireplace. "Do you mind, Master?" he asked. "My old bones feel the cold more than they used to. And being rousted from bed in the middle of the night doesn't help." But he smiled when he said it.

"Middle of the night?" Seb retorted. "At this time in London I would still be getting dressed to go out."

"That's as may be, but things have gone from bad to worse at Albury House. There's not enough money to cover the cost of running a house this size and not much hope of things improving when the estate has gone to rack and ruin."

Sebastian was silent. This was news indeed.

Catherine cleared her throat, and Seb realized he was being a bad host again and made haste to introduce her. "Grimsley, this is the Dowager Duchess of Winstanton. She is in need of our hospitality for the night. I've asked for rooms to be prepared."

Grimsley looked at her with interest. "Your Grace," he said politely. "I have heard of you, of course, even though I've never laid eyes on you before now."

Catherine smiled wryly. "My late husband was not one for visiting neighbors, Mr. Grimsley."

Grimsley made a sound of agreement, before returning his attention to Sebastian. "I'm glad you came home," he said, and there was an urgency in his tone that made Seb frown. "You're right, your father isn't dying. His body is as hale and hearty as ever. But his mind . . ." He shook his head. "Things can't go on as they have been. We need you here to take charge."

"His mind?" Seb repeated quietly. "Is that why the house—"

"Oh, he'll know you. Don't worry that he won't. But these days . . . he's returned to the past. Maybe he prefers it there, Master Sebastian."

Seb rubbed a hand against his chest, as though that might soothe the ache. Grimsley's words sounded ominous. The past was something Seb always preferred to avoid, and he had done his best to avoid it for twelve years now. But his father needed him, Grimsley needed him, Albury House needed him, and it seemed the time had come for Sebastian to stop running.

Chapter Twenty-One

THE BEDCHAMBER HAD a stale smell that suggested it had not been in use for some time. But once Maggie had changed and aired the bedding and lit candles, everything felt so much better. Catherine sighed as she sat in the chair before the looking glass while her maid brushed out her hair. She felt travel stained and weary, but a bath could only be a dream at this point. It had been a long day and despite dozing in the coach on the way here, all she wanted to do was sleep.

But her mind was racing.

"This is a strange household," Maggie said. "If I did not know the earl lived here, I would wonder if it was abandoned. That sitting room . . . nothing had been touched for years."

"It was Sebastian's mother's room."

Maggie was right, time had stopped here when the countess died, and the clock had never started again. Sebastian had looked shocked when he understood the situation. Had he known how matters stood, would he have come home sooner?

"I'm not sure I would want to stay here for longer than a night." Maggie finished braiding Catherine's hair.

"Then it's just as well we're not," Catherine replied tartly. "We will be leaving as early as possible in the morning."

Maggie met her eyes in the mirror. "And Dodds is coming

with us."

At least there was that.

When Catherine climbed beneath the covers, she discovered that Maggie had warmed them with a warming pan, and weary tears stung her eyes. "Thank you," she said. "I appreciate your care of me, Maggie. I don't think I say that enough."

Maggie's grin was awry, as if she too was feeling the emotion of the moment. "What would you do without me, eh, my lady?"

Catherine knew that one day soon she may have to learn to do without her maid. But that was a worry for another time, and right now she needed to sleep.

Earlier, in the sitting room, Sebastian had held her in his arms. There was nothing sexual about it, just a craving for comfort and closeness. She had wanted to comfort him and he seemed to need her close. Seeing Sebastian so vulnerable . . . how could she not hold him and try to make things better?

It was too late, and she was too tired, to unravel the tangle of her emotions. She was just falling asleep when a knock on her door woke her. She wanted to ignore it, but a number of worrying possibilities had her rising from her bed to open it. Catherine should have been surprised to see Sebastian standing there, the candle in his hand illuminating his face and accentuating the lines about his mouth and the shadows beneath his eyes. She should have been surprised, but she wasn't.

"Apologies," he said. "I thought you might be asleep by now, but I . . . I wanted to make sure you were comfortable."

"I am," she assured him. When he didn't move, staring down at her, she asked, "What is it? Sebastian?"

The candle flame wavered with his breath. "Can I . . . may I stay for a little while? Not for anything . . . just to be with you."

She might have thought it an odd request, if not for the way he had held her in the sitting room. The closeness and the comfort.

Without a word she stepped back from the door. Her feet felt frozen and hurriedly she climbed back into bed, dragging up the covers to her chin, and watching him over the top of them. Sebastian set down the candle, the flame dancing in a draft from the windows, which the thin curtains did little to keep out.

"I didn't realize things were so bad," he said, waving a hand to encompass the room. "I would never have asked you here if I had known."

She reminded him, "I have lived in worse. You forget, I wasn't always a duchess. We were very poor after my father died. And I'm glad you did ask me, because it means I will be home for my son's birthday."

He had taken off his boots and was standing in his stockinged feet, breeches, and shirt sleeves. She thought he was probably cold, too, and before she thought about it too deeply, she said, "Come to bed. If you like we can talk here."

He didn't even hesitate before he climbed in beside her. "Thank you," he said with a sigh. "I don't know why it is, but when I am with you I feel calmer. And by God I need to be calm right now, Catherine."

His words warmed her. She wanted to tell him that when she was with him she felt calmer too. And safer. He made her feel safe from the world at large, as if she had found the perfect harbor with him. As if he cared for her and would protect her.

They laid their heads on the pillows together and looked up at the canopy above. It was an old bed, probably as old as the house, and no doubt had many tales to tell. Although this would surely be one of the strangest.

"I wanted to tell you about my mother," he said after a moment.

"Sebastian, you don't have to."

"I want to," he said quietly. "I think I told Dodds once, when I was drunk, but no one else. Until now there was no one I wanted to tell. Is that," he paused, sounding almost shy, "is that all right?"

She squeezed his fingers in hers. "Of course it is." Catherine turned on her side, watching him. He did not look at her, his gaze on the canopy above, and he seemed to be finding the right words.

"She wanted to ride in the gig. She had made up some tale about a dragon, and that we had to escape it. She was like that. Full of fun and stories, full of life. Every day was a new and exciting chapter. Not always, of course. There were times when she was despondent, so low that my father feared for her. We crept about the house and dared not open the curtains. And then slowly, slowly, she would come back to us."

"You loved her all the more because of her fragility."

He turned to her and smiled. "Yes. You understand. I knew you would." Then he sighed. "That day in the gig—. We called it the suicide gig because it was so high off the ground, and not very stable, but she loved it. She said it felt like we were flying. I always insisted on driving, although..." His eyes looked far away, and he was back there, living the memory. "Father never wanted her to drive, but sometimes I let her. Not this day. I said no, and she was annoyed with me, but I could tell she was in a particularly reckless mood. She kept insisting I drive faster. We went through the village in a flash and everyone stared. She was laughing, shouting for me to drive faster and faster, that the dragon would catch us. And then—." He swallowed and looked up at the canopy. "She tried to take the reins from me, but I wouldn't let her have them. I think there was a ditch, and it threw us off balance and we tipped, and then it was all over. She was killed and I survived."

"Not your fault," she said gently. "But you know that."

"My father made it my fault. I tried to tell him that I was careful, that I kept hold of the reins, but he wouldn't listen. He sent me away."

They were silent. She wanted to say something that would make everything better, but what could she say? Besides, she thought that listening was enough. "Thank you," she said softly, "for telling me."

He wiped his eyes, and then cleared his throat. "I think I will have to stay here at Albury House," he said. "My father . . ." He shook his head. "I will know more tomorrow, but I wanted to tell you, in case . . ." Again he turned his head to look at her and she met his eyes, waiting. "In case you need me," he finished.

Catherine felt something inside her still. Did he mean . . . ? What *did* he mean? "Need you?"

He reached for her hand, fumbling beneath the covers. "I meant if you need to talk to me. If you need my help. Winstanton is not the place for you, but I understand why you have to stay. I just wanted you to know I would be here if you ever needed me."

He was being kind. Even though he wasn't offering her the love she craved, he was thinking of her and offering her his support. No man had ever done that before.

"Thank you," she whispered. Then, as he moved toward the side of the bed, "Please, stay."

He glanced back at her and some of the old teasing was in his smile. "I was just going to blow out the candle."

He did and she felt him settle back in beside her. Soon his breathing steadied, and she followed him into sleep.

At some point in the night she became aware of his strong arm about her waist, and his warm breath fanning her nape. His body was curved around hers, like a spoon. It felt perfect, and without another thought she drifted once more into sleep.

This time the sound of low voices woke her.

"Father? What are you doing here?" Sebastian was trying to whisper. He sounded shocked.

Startled into full wakefulness, Catherine raised her head. The room was still shadowy, but it must be morning because she could see a little. There was an older man standing beside the bed on Sebastian's side. His hair looked almost the same color as Sebastian's in this light, but she had a feeling it was white rather than fair. However, there was no mistaking those pale eyes. He glanced across at her, seeming to notice her for the first time, but immediately turned back to his son.

"Did you have another nightmare?" he asked Sebastian gently, in the voice one would use when talking to a distressed child. "You know you can always come to me."

Sebastian didn't seem to know what to say.

The earl went on. "I know it's early, but I thought we could take a look at the wood." He shifted from foot to foot. He seemed unable to keep still, his excitement making him jittery. "The trees are so tall now and I want you to see them."

Sebastian sat up and, with a glance at Catherine, said, "Isn't it a little early to be visiting the wood?"

"Nonsense," his father retorted. "Things are always better when it's early. The world is so much fresher, the day so new. I like to think that anything is possible."

Sebastian hesitated and then seemed to make up his mind. "All right. Just let me get dressed. My clothes are . . ." He looked about him, as if remembering this wasn't his room. "Come with me, Father," he said firmly.

The earl gave Catherine one more puzzled glance before he followed his son docilely to the door. It closed after them.

Catherine flung herself back on the mattress and stared at the ceiling. What on earth! Was this what Grimsley had meant? The earl appeared to believe his son was still a child. That gentleness in his voice . . .

Tears burned her eyes. This wasn't the atrocious father she had imagined, the one who had banished his son and refused to have any contact with him for years. Sebastian had suffered all this time and now, faced with the reality of the situation, he must be very confused.

Catherine rubbed her eyes and yawned, and then unexpectedly she giggled. This was not the start to the day she had expected, but when it came to Albury House nothing seemed quite normal.

Quickly she sobered. Today she must go home. Jack would be waiting. He was probably worried she would miss his birthday, but as long as she arrived before midnight she would find some way to cheer him up. Perhaps they could have a picnic in his bedchamber? Something unexpected, something a little like

Sebastian's mother might have come up with.

She would never forget last night, how Sebastian had come to her and held her in his arms as they slept. It had felt right, like they could face anything together. Would she ever take advantage of his offer? Would she come to him if she needed a friendly ear? The thought of leaving Winstanton behind, even for a day or two, was soothing.

But at the same time she wondered, if she came to him, how could she bear leaving him again? Better not to come at all, if it would make her life at the castle even more lonely and difficult.

She found the bellpull and heard the summons jangling deep in the house. Once Maggie came, they must be on their way. Jack was her priority now, and she refused to think of anything else.

Chapter Twenty-Two

SEBASTIAN FOLLOWED HIS father through the old knot garden. Like everything else it was neglected and overgrown, and the hedges that had always been so precisely trimmed were all out of alignment. He remembered how in the warmer weather the spicy scent of herbs had filled the air. Now everything was stark, only a few buds here and there. Stone walls which had been built to protect the more tender plants from the harsh weather were in disrepair. There was the bench where Sebastian had often sat with his mother.

He opened his mouth to share the memory with his father but closed it again. This was not the man who had shouted at him and sent him away. His father seemed younger in a strange way, despite looking older. And if he remembered anything of that awful day when Seb left, he did not show it. When Seb had mentioned something about his home in London, his father had given him a blank stare. It was almost as though, in the earl's mind, Seb had never left Albury House.

Was Grimsley right when he said the earl was happier in the past?

Seb wondered how long this had been going on, because now they were out in the pre-dawn light and he could see his father properly, he noticed the neglect. Just like the house and garden, the earl hadn't been cared for in some time. His father had always been so dedicated when it came to his duties as master of Albury House, so particular in everything he did, but he was not that man anymore.

Was the estate in as bad a way as Grimsley said? One good thing about his years in London: Seb had made enough money to turn things around.

As Seb had expected, the trees in the wood were bare, with snow still in patches on the ground from the recent storm. None of this stopped his father from marching onward, pointing out this tree or that. He was talking quickly and Seb only caught one word in ten. Besides, his own thoughts were racing just as quickly and it was difficult to concentrate.

But when he heard his mother's name his ears pricked up.

"Your grandfather did not want me to marry Eloise. He said she was unstable, that the whole family was unhinged. Her mother was known for her moods, melancholic one moment and bouncing about the next. But I didn't care about that. My heart yearned for her. I loved her."

"We both loved her," Seb said quietly. There were whole weeks when his mother would lay in bed with the curtains drawn, but they were followed by an almost inhuman energy. Waking Seb up at midnight so that they could climb to the top of the house and look at the stars from the roof, or dancing about the garden in the moonlight—he had thought it normal if he thought about it at all. It was normal to him. He was proud of her; she wasn't like any of his school friends' mothers. She wasn't like anyone else in the whole world, and when she wasn't melancholy she took such joy in life.

"We did love her." His father nodded and patted his arm. "How could we not?"

When Seb had realized his father was living in the past, he had worried the earl might believe his wife was still alive and would be seeking her. But it wasn't like that. He knew Eloise was gone, and Seb was grateful for that, even if he was confused by the holes in his father's understanding.

"You are like me, Sebastian," his father said, turning to him with a smile. "I am glad of that. As much as I loved your mother, I would not want you to suffer as she did during those bad times. You have been blessed with my good sense and even temperament."

Seb was too surprised to reply. The earl didn't seem to notice. He tilted his head back and looked up into the branches of the large tree before them. "Come on," he said matter-of-factly, "give me a hand up."

Startled, Seb did as he was told, and watched in disbelief as his elderly father began to climb the tree. Reaching up to take hold of a branch and then hauling himself onto it, and then reaching up again. He was far more nimble than he looked, but Seb hurried to follow him, worried he was going to slip and fall.

"I don't think you should . . ." he began breathlessly, but his father wasn't listening.

"There is an amazing view from the top. Your mother showed it to me before we were married. Wait and see."

There was nothing Seb could do but follow, taking care with his handholds and the slippery bark beneath his boots. He wasn't dressed for tree climbing. Before long they were at the top, swaying a little with the breeze, while the sun rose before them, sending its golden light across the land.

"There," his father said, beaming. "Beautiful, isn't it?"

It was. This was his home, and he had missed it. Only now did he admit to himself that his life in London had always felt temporary. He was an exile, longing for home. Cautiously, Seb turned and looked back at the house, with its quaint additions and many windows. There was a commotion on the drive, and he could see that his coach had been brought around and Catherine and Maggie were about to climb inside. Dodds was there, rushing about, seeing to their luggage.

Last night he had held Catherine in his arms. Who would have thought a practiced rake like Albury could be satisfied with such a thing?

Seb continued to watch as they moved away, slowly at first and then gaining speed. Catherine was leaving and he felt her loss painfully. As if something was missing and it could not be returned until she was with him again.

Beside him his father was speaking in a dreamy voice. "Always follow your heart. Don't let anyone try to dissuade you. Even if your happiness doesn't last as long as you would wish it to, that is better than spending your life never having known it at all."

The earl was not speaking to Seb about Catherine, he knew that, but right then he felt like he was.

Chapter Twenty-Three

IT WAS ANOTHER long day's journey. At least the sun was shining, which made even the rocky moors around Winstanton seem moderately welcoming. Maggie was quiet, glancing out of the coach now and again to make sure Dodds was still riding beside them. Grimsley had arranged for them to have some food packed for the journey, and Catherine was grateful for that. She had not seen Sebastian before they left—he was evidently still with his father—and now she wondered if she would ever see him again.

The thought left her shaky, but she steadied herself. Soon she would be with Jack.

When they finally reached the castle, it was well and truly dark. As the coach drew to a halt, Catherine was reminded of their arrival last night at Albury House. The torch that was usually placed in the sconce by the door hadn't been lit, and Dodds used one of the coach lanterns to show them the way. Catherine's body was aching from the journey despite the modern equipage. Yes, it had been a great deal quicker than her own ancient vehicle, but she would have preferred not to have spent so long inside it.

Ellinor would usually have heard them arrive and come to meet them, but there was no sign of her and no one to answer the heavy door knocker. When Catherine pushed her hands against the heavy weight of it in frustration, it opened without resistance. That was also strange and worrying. Inside, the vast entrance hall was all shadows, but there was a faint light on the table at the top of the staircase.

Dodds and Maggie hurried ahead to find the housekeeper, while Catherine took up the light and made her way to Jack's room. To her consternation his door *was* locked. Anxiously, she rattled at the handle, calling his name, and a moment later he responded.

"Mama? Mama!" His voice sounded croaky, like he had a cold. Or had been crying in there all alone.

"Where is the key, Jack? Why did Ellinor lock you in?"

His answer was slightly garbled, but she made shocking sense of it. It turned out that Ellinor had fallen two days ago and hurt herself, and the elderly staff could not look after her and a young child who seemed determined to keep running out of the castle to watch for his mother. So they had locked him in.

Maggie returned, breathless, with the housekeeper, Mrs. Howard. When Catherine began to demand how she could have locked Jack in his room, the woman appeared unrepentant. Tight-lipped, she took the key from the bundle at her waist and the next moment Jack flung himself into Catherine's arms.

"See, no harm done," Mrs. Howard said briskly.

"I had a candle but it—it burned down, Mama! You know I don't like the dark."

Catherine glared at the housekeeper over her son's head.

Mrs. Howard sniffed. "He kept running off, my lady. And then Miss Ellinor was so ill. I couldn't be having it. I'm not as young as I used to be."

Catherine was furious as she comforted Jack, but she restrained herself. There was no point in starting an argument now. The morning would do, when she was settled and Jack had calmed down. She knew how old the housekeeper was, but it was difficult to forgive her when presented with her little son's damp, woebegone face.

"It was my birthday," he wailed, "and you promised. I waited and waited but you didn't come."

It broke her heart as she kissed his flushed cheeks, sticky with tears, and tried to soothe him. "I'm here now," she said, "and I have presents for you. Wait until you see them."

That helped a little, but every now and again he would give a hiccupped sob and cling to her, while the housekeeper looked on disapprovingly. Catherine could imagine what she was thinking: Spare the rod and spoil the child. Well, too bad. She would spoil Jack as much as she liked and no one was going to stop her.

Dodds appeared behind Maggie, a frown on his face. Mrs. Howard eyed him warily, but he ignored her and said to Catherine, "Your Grace, I am told your sister-in-law is calling for you."

"I forgot about her," Maggie exclaimed. "That's what I came to tell you, my lady. Miss Ellinor wants you."

With Jack's hand clasped firmly in hers, Catherine followed Maggie to Ellinor's bedchamber.

The candlelight made shadows, but the room was warm and cozy in comparison to Jack's, where there had been no light or fire. Her sister-in-law was seated in a chair by the hearth. She started to get up when Catherine entered but groaned and fell back. Catherine could see that her swollen foot was propped up on a stack of cushions.

"I fell over," she said irritably. "I was rushing and tripped over the carpet runner, and I fell. I was lucky it was just a sprain." Then, with a frown, "I was expecting you back days ago, Catherine."

"The storm made it impossible to travel," Catherine responded woodenly. Then, with a glance at the listening housekeeper, "Thank you, Mrs. Howard, that will be all."

The woman hesitated, obviously preferring to stay, and then closed the door behind her. Catherine sat down on the straight-backed chair beside Ellinor, and Jack climbed onto her lap. He was sucking his thumb, something he had not done for years, and that worried her. She put her arms around him and held him close.

"You were supposed to be back for Jack's birthday," Ellinor said accusingly, her eyes going from the child to its mother. "He was most upset."

"Mrs. Howard locked him in his bedroom."

Ellinor's eyes widened. "I—I did not know."

"She said she was run off her feet with looking after you and did not have time for him, which I suppose is true, but Jack does not understand that. And I do not condone it. The room was dark, and he has been weeping in there for hours. What would have happened if I hadn't come home tonight?"

Ellinor looked pale. "I didn't know," she whispered. "I did not ask her to do that."

Catherine took a breath. "Of course you didn't, but it happened nevertheless."

"Poor little worm," Maggie said, patting Jack's head.

He looked up and tried to smile at her, but instead gave another hiccup.

"Have you had any cake yet?" Maggie demanded, hands on her hips. "Well, come with me little master and I will find you something fit for a birthday boy."

Catherine smiled, watching as Jack reached for Maggie's hand. He loved her and trusted her, and she was more grateful than ever for her maid. And then Ellinor interrupted the tender moment.

"You should call him Your Grace."

Catherine turned to her. The tightly pursed mouth, the narrowed eyes—in the firelight she looked very much like her brother. Ellinor, who had been giving Maggie a stern look, now seemed to sense Catherine's anger and turned back to her.

"Jack is the duke and the people around him must learn to defer to him as is only right and proper. You do not understand these things, Catherine. You are a commoner."

Catherine wasn't sure which of her emotions was the strongest. Anger at her son being turned into a figurehead and denied the affection a little boy needed, or her sister-in-law's obliviousness. She shouldn't have been surprised. Ellinor was a product of her family. She did not understand loneliness other than as something that must be overcome, in the hope it would eventually make one stronger.

"I thought you were better than your brother," she managed to say, her voice trembling, "but you are worse."

Maggie, still waiting, caught her breath.

Ellinor's gaze widened, and then narrowed. "I am Jack's guardian," she said, a threat against what she must see in Catherine's eyes. "I warn you—"

"Do your worst," Catherine said, and stood up. "Jack and I are leaving. Maggie, can you pack him a bag? And tell Dodds I am sorry but we must leave immediately."

Maggie's eyes shone as she led Jack to the door. "That is not soon enough."

"And don't let Mrs. Howard stop you," Catherine called after her, and heard Maggie's snort of laughter drift back.

"You don't know what you're doing!" Ellinor said, and there was desperation as well as anger in her voice. "*Think* what you are doing! Will Jack thank you when he learns what your ignorance has cost him?"

The words worked on that anxiety she had had ever since she read the will, but then Catherine remembered her son, sobbing in his cold, dark, locked room, with no one to help him.

"I am never leaving him again," she said.

Ellinor seemed to relax. She took a breath. "Good, I am glad you see sense."

"Because he is coming with me."

"With you!" Ellinor screeched. "With you where?"

"Albury House," Catherine said over her shoulder, on her way to the door. "I am going to Viscount Albury."

She did not hear what Ellinor replied, her words were mangled with rage and thwarted desire as she tried to stand up on her injured foot. Catherine told herself she should feel at least a little sorry for the woman, but she didn't. She felt an overwhelming relief. She was doing the right thing. She was taking her son away from this place to give him a happier life, and if he was disappointed with her in later years . . . well, she would face that then, but she did not think Jack would be disappointed. She would make certain he was not.

Albury would take them in. She trusted him to keep his word, and then she would travel south to London. To her mother and sisters. She would find shelter there, and when the gossip had died down, then she would think about her future. Hers and Jack's.

Chapter Twenty-Four

DODDS ARRIVED FIRST, his horse panting and blowing, his ugly face bright with the exciting news. Seb stood and heard him out, wondering at first whether his manservant had lost his mind. Catherine had left Winstanton with her son and was coming to Albury? She had broken the terms of the will. She would receive nothing now, and Jack would be disinherited from his property and fortune, left with nothing but an empty title. It was tragic.

Seb grinned.

"And she's coming here?" He had given her the invitation to visit him whenever she needed to, but this was far sooner than he had expected. Not that he was complaining, and when Dodds explained the circumstances, he grew angry.

"She means to go on to her mother in London," Dodds added, with a sly look.

"Does she?"

Seb looked away, toward the wood. His father was in there, planting more trees. The most recent storm had knocked a few more over and the earl was determined to replace them. Seb had been helping him until Dodds' arrival.

The past two days had been very strange. He had his father back, and he wasn't sure how to feel about that. Should he be glad that the earl's mind was disturbed, because it meant they could be together again, or should he insist on discussing that awful time, reminding his father why his son had been banished?

"Let it be," Grimsley had advised him, woolly eyebrows wriggling independently. "If he remembers, *then* you can worry about it, but if he doesn't . . . enjoy the time you have with him." The old man gave him a stern look. "Will you be returning to London, Master Sebastian?"

Sebastian met the look and smiled. "No, I won't. I'm needed here."

And now Catherine was coming and it felt like this was another chance he had thought he would never have. Was he going to grasp it with both hands, or let her go south and slip away from him?

It was after noon when the coach arrived. They had started out very late last night, after Catherine refused to spend another night in the castle. This time Seb made sure there were refreshments and the rooms were properly prepared. The housekeeper had returned from her enforced stay at her sisters' home, and soon taken over the smooth running of the house.

"I'm so glad to see you back, Master Sebastian," she had said, her eyes suspiciously bright. "We've missed you. The earl has missed you too, though he'd never admit it. Even before he became ill, he knew in his heart it wasn't your fault, what happened to your mother, but he had to blame someone, anyone, who wasn't her. He loved her so much and sometimes love makes people willfully blind."

Seb didn't know what to think, whether to believe her words or dismiss them as wishful thinking. And what did it matter anyway? Yes, he had suffered, and the years had been difficult, but it had not been all bad. He had lived a life he would never have lived at Albury House if he had stayed, and he would never have met Catherine. It made his heart sore to think they could have lived their whole lives separated by a day's travel and never known each other. But he *had* met her and maybe he was being arrogant, but he wasn't going to deny himself this chance to keep her.

As he watched the coach come to a halt on the drive, he was filled with resolve.

Seb strode forward and opened the coach door before the footman could touch it, standing with his hand out to help her down. She looked up at him, and he saw she was utterly spent.

Her lips trembled. "I'm sorry," she whispered. "I didn't know where else to go."

Seb reached in and lifted her out, cradling her in his arms, and then he kissed her. She wrapped her arm about his neck and clung, kissing him back. He wanted to keep kissing her, and he might have done so, if they were not interrupted by a small boy shouting.

"Leave my mother alone!"

Gently Seb put Catherine down, and she took the boy in her arms, holding him close, before setting him back so that she could look into his eyes.

"Jack, this is Viscount Albury. This is his house, and he has kindly offered for us to stay here for a while."

"He was *kissing* you," Jack said in disgust.

"My apologies, Your Grace," Seb swept the boy and his mother an elegant bow.

Jack stared up at him uncertainly. Now that Seb could see him clearly, he was very much like his mother, with dark hair and eyes, and bidding to be a handsome man one day. But he looked frightened too, and sad, and Seb knew what that felt like.

"Now young master, you be nice to the viscount," Maggie scolded. "You'll like it here."

"We're not staying," Catherine hurriedly added, looking at Seb.

Did she mean that? Her eyes were just as sad as her son's, and suddenly Seb felt overwhelmed with that emotion he knew now was love. It swooped in and filled him up, and it was powerful and frightening, and at the same time quite wonderful.

"I want you to stay," he said quietly. "Please stay. Stay forever."

Catherine didn't seem to know what to say to him. Perhaps she was overwhelmed too. Tears filled her eyes, but before they could fall, a voice called out to them.

"Sebastian, who have we here?"

His father walked toward them, his hands dirty from planting his trees, and a welcoming smile on his face. "Who is this young chap then?"

"I am the Duke of Winstanton," Jack replied grandly, and then shot a doubtful look at his mother. "I still am, aren't I, Mama?"

"Yes, you are," she assured him, quickly wiping beneath her eyes. "Jack, this is the Earl of Eltham, and he's Sebast . . . the viscount's father."

"Well, well, I need some help, young man. I have trees to plant. In the years to come they will grow big and strong, like my son here. Like you. Will you help me?"

Jack looked hopefully at his mother, and she nodded with a smile. He set off with the earl, glancing back once or twice. After a moment Seb's father paused and held out his hand, and tentatively Jack placed his in it. A moment later he giggled at something the earl said, and he didn't look back again.

"Will he be all right?" Catherine asked anxiously, watching them go.

"Perfectly. Although . . ." Seb remembered how his father had climbed that tree. "Perhaps Grimsley can go with them. Just to make sure there is no tree climbing involved."

The old man, who had been observing them with a smile, now began to follow.

Dodds and Maggie slipped away, and Catherine and Seb stood alone in front of the house that would one day be his. He took a deep breath. It was time for honesty. By telling her the truth he had nothing to lose and everything to gain.

"I love you," he said. The words gave him an overwhelming sense of joy. "I love you," he said it again.

Catherine was staring up at him. "Sebastian . . ."

He smiled a smile he knew was far from his practiced ones. Full of doubt and hope. He had so much to say. "Love. I'm still getting used to it. I don't expect you to love me back, Catherine. I know you have every reason to be wary of me. But if you will stay here with me, I solemnly promise to dedicate my life to you and Jack. I will never hurt you, I will never grow tired of you— the very idea is ridiculous. I will give you everything you need. Everything you want."

Her eyes were bright with tears, and she gave a sort of gasping laugh. "I never thought to hear those words from you. I think I knew you felt them, but you seemed so determined to carry on with your life in London . . ."

"I'm sorry," he whispered. "I needed a little time to . . . adjust. I'm ready now."

She stepped closer to him and rested her hands on his shoulders, smoothing the fine cloth with her fingers as she gazed into his face. Searching. Reading him. And he stood and let her see every thought and emotion passing through him, because he no longer had anything to hide.

Her smile made her eyes shine, with happiness this time rather than tears. "I love you, too. It seems impossible, but I think I loved you from the moment I saw you ten years ago. When you offered to run away with me. Over the years I've always hoped you would make good on that offer."

He threw his head back and laughed aloud. "Do you mean if I had arrived at the doors of your castle, you would have let me ride away with you?"

She smiled back at him. "I rather think I would. Jack, too, of course." Her smile faded slightly, as if the thought of her son made her anxious. Seb made haste to reassure her on that matter.

"Jack is more than welcome in my home. I will enjoy getting to know him. I am an expert in making snowmen now."

She looked as though she might cry again, so he bent his head and kissed her, enjoying the sensation of her soft lips beneath his.

"Sebastian," she breathed.

"We should marry as soon as possible," he said, and began to carefully kiss every freckle on her adorable nose. "Do you think Jack will give his consent?"

"I think you will win him over. He'll love you just as I do."

He tried not to let her see how much that meant to him, but as usual he failed. She wound her arms about his neck and tugged to bring him closer, and then she kissed him breathless.

When he was able to, he looked about them, only just realizing they were still standing on the drive. No doubt giving everyone a nice show. Well, who cared? He was the happiest man in the world and he didn't care who knew it.

"You will marry me then, Catherine? You will stay here with me and be my love for as long as we live?"

Catherine rested her cheek against his shoulder in perfect contentment. "With all my heart, Sebastian."

Epilogue

Three months later

CATHERINE CLOSED HER eyes and lay back in the bed. The wedding had gone off without a hitch, and even her mother was satisfied with the bridegroom. He may not be a duke but one day he would be an earl. Not that it mattered to Catherine. He was Sebastian to her, and she loved him with every part of her being.

He was still downstairs, receiving congratulations from their friends and neighbors. Actually, there were a lot of both, something she had never realized when she lived at Winstanton. She had asked Ellinor to the wedding but her sister-in-law hadn't come. It seemed a pity she could not put the past behind her, but Catherine supposed it was to be expected. The late duke's word would always be law.

Jack had been wary for a while after they arrived at Albury House, but as she knew he would, Sebastian won him over. The turning point had been when Jack saw some puppies in the village, and Seb had presented him with one. Catherine did not think she had ever seen her son so deliriously happy.

Maggie and Dodds were married now and living in one of the cottages on the estate, although they insisted on retaining their positions with Sebastian and Catherine until they had trained up suitable replacements. The list of requirements for those replacements seemed very long and detailed, and Catherine doubted such paragons existed.

The bedchamber door opened and closed, interrupting her thoughts.

"Ah, here she is, my beautiful, delicious wife." Catherine laughed as Sebastian strolled toward her, stripping off his shirt, and tossing it aside, and then unbuttoning his breeches. He really did look as if he wanted to eat her up.

When he reached her and knelt on the side of the bed, she tugged him down on top of her. His mouth closed eagerly on hers, their tongues battling. They had become very good at kissing over the past three months, and now they kissed for a long time. Until Catherine was boneless and hot and aching in all the right places.

"It is time to recommence your lessons," he said, his voice husky as he ran his finger down the opening of the silken robe she was wearing.

She looked up at him through her lashes. "I can't wait, husband," she said in a breathless voice.

When he parted the robe and saw she was naked, he groaned. He bent to gently suck on the rosy tip of first one breast, and then the other. Catherine slid her hands over his broad shoulders, cupping the muscles as she leaned up for more kisses.

"You are very needy, wife," he said with mock severity. "But I have the solution."

He rolled her over, so that she was on top, and her loose hair fell about them, making a cave. Her breasts were too tempting, and he licked and nipped, and she wriggled so that his hard length was where she needed it. She began to move, rubbing herself against his cock over and over again. It felt so good, and she had missed this so much. She could reach her climax by simply doing this, and perhaps she would have done so, but he held her still.

"Not yet my needy wife," he said, and she could hear the

amusement behind the words.

He reached down between them, his fingers gliding past the dark curls at the juncture of her thighs, caressing her swollen folds, groaning at her wetness. Her body rippled about him in bliss. Once more she thought she was going to climax, and he must have known it, because he stopped, and smiled up at her. "It has been too long. I will need to have you at least three times before my cock softens enough to walk."

She burst into laughter, muffling the sound against the curve of his neck and shoulder. Happiness bubbled in her blood, mixing with desire.

For three months they had resisted intercourse, waiting until they were wed, not wanting to scandalize anyone more than they already had. Catherine's mother had traveled north to stay with them as her daughter's chaperone, although Catherine suspected if she had pushed the point her mother would have turned a blind eye. But there was Jack to think of, settling him into his new life at Albury House, and making sure he knew how welcome he was.

Sebastian had suffered during their weeks of abstention. And every time their paths crossed in Albury House he had stopped to kiss her.

"Why did we agree to this?" he had whispered.

"Because your father wanted the wedding to be the beginning of our lives together and not just a continuation of what we already had." Catherine had repeated the words—she had memorised them by then. She had giggled when he groaned like a man in agony and rested his head on her shoulder.

"I suffer. Take pity on me." He had placed her hand on the large bulge in his breeches. "Suck me."

"Oh, I will," she had promised him, "when we are wed, my love."

But for all her amusement, Catherine had suffered as much as Sebastian. During their time at The White Rose Inn he had lit a fire inside her, and it continued to smolder. She wanted him almost more than she could bear, but she also knew the earl was right. Their marriage should be the beginning, a new start to the rest of their lives.

And now they were wed.

His thumb circled her swollen pearl with an expertise that had her whimpering in urgent need. She nuzzled against his jaw, licking, tasting him. As she lay on his bigger body she indulged herself, rubbing her aching breasts against the hairs on his muscular chest, pushing against his hand.

He whispered in her ear. "Take me inside you, Catherine. Fuck me."

It took a moment for the words to make sense. She lifted her head and looked down at him. "You want me to . . .?"

He grinned. "Up you get." He helped her to sit up. She pressed her palms against his chest, using him for balance, and straddled his narrow hips. His cock was right there in front of her, irresistible, so she bent down and gave it a lick.

He shuddered. "*Now* she sucks me," he moaned. "As much as I enjoy your mouth, my love, I will hold strong this time. I want to be inside you. Ride me, use me."

Catherine used her knees to lift herself up. His cock was throbbing in her hand, and desire flared in his pale eyes as he raised his head so that he could see her body and his. She moved over him and pressed the tip to her aching core.

"Yes," he groaned.

Slowly she pressed down onto him, feeling her body stretching to take that rigid, velvet-covered flesh. Before she had taken him all the way he pushed up, deep inside her, his hips arching, his hands clasping her thighs. Pleasure sent hot bolts through her.

For a moment they were so eager they were a little clumsy, but soon they found their rhythm. It felt so good, but she couldn't make it last, not this time. At one point Sebastian sat up, so that she was on his lap, but they kept moving. Quickly now, as the top of the mountain rose before them, and then they flew over the peak. She cried out and he echoed her.

It took a long moment to regain her breath and her senses. They were lying together now, him holding her close against his side, his seed sticky between her legs. Idly, she wondered if they would have children together, but that thought was for another day.

He tucked her hair out of her face and brushed his nose against her, breathing her in. "I love you," he said.

She smiled and kissed him. "Hmm, I love you, too, my dearest rake."

He gave a wicked laugh. "The things we are going to do together. The life we are going to have."

And she smiled again because it sounded like a pledge. And a promise.

About the Author

Sara Bennett is an Australian bestselling author of Historical Romance. She has written many books set in various time periods—Medieval, Regency and Victorian—as well as Paranormal Romance under the name Sara Mackenzie.

She started her career writing under the penname Deborah Miles for Mills & Boon. Her books have been published by Avon/Harper Collins, and are available worldwide. She has also written numerous Australian Women's Fiction books as Kaye Dobbie. Currently she alternates between publishing independently and with traditional publishers.

Sara has been a finalist for the RITA award (Romance Writers of America) and the RUBY (Romance Writers of Australia).

Sara lives in Victoria, Australia, in an old house in a goldrush town, with her husband and two important cats. She would love to spend more time in the garden but there are just too many stories to be written.